C000185623

INSIDE
OUT

INSIDE OUT

NATALIE HIBBERD

Matador
9 Priory Business Park,
Wistow Road, Kibworth Beauchamp,
Leicestershire, LE8 0RX
Tel: 0116 279 2299
Email: books@troubador.co.uk
Web: www.troubador.co.uk/matador
Twitter: @matadorbooks

ISBN 978 1838590 604

British Library Cataloguing in Publication Data.
A catalogue record for this book is available from the British Library.

Printed and bound in Great Britain by 4edge Limited
Typeset in 11pt Minion Pro by Troubador Publishing Ltd, Leicester, UK

Matador is an imprint of Troubador Publishing Ltd

*For Mum, who heard my stories first,
and for Dad, who saved this one from the
jaws of certain death.*

*This book is also dedicated to the
memory of Joan Harcourt
(1st December 1927 – 26th March 2012)*

ONE

Zack McGregor stifled a yawn of exhaustion and sat back in his chair. Why was life so complicated nowadays? Rain was bucketing down, launching a vicious onslaught upon the windows and adding considerably to the intensity of his headache. He let out a moan of protest and half-closed his eyes; he was *so* tired!

Zack, though only sixteen, had been employed for a long time as major-domo and clerk to Samuel Brand – the prime minister of The Inside. A flash of lightning illuminated the stuffy box room Zack called his office and the half-finished speech he was writing for Samuel, which was lying on the oaken desk. He sighed heavily, picked it up and reread what he'd written:

The so-called Freedom Fighters [the FF] shall not prevail; they are nothing but cowards who feel that violence is the way to achieve what they want: control and ownership of The Inside. We will ensure that this does not happen.

Despite the constant threats we have received, we have not given in to the outrageous demands of an organisation that is so hell bent on destroying the time of peace and prosperity we have all worked so hard to achieve.

He screwed the paper into a ball, sighed again, then tossed it over his shoulder into the metal waste paper bin in the corner. It was no good; it just wasn't right. For one thing, the Freedom Fighters' 'outrageous demands' had resulted in the receipt of substantial sums of ransom money on more than one occasion, with the most recent payout being just last week. The terrorist group had threatened to plant a bomb in the Golden Crown Shopping Centre at the height of the midday rush. This would have killed hundreds of people. For another thing, it felt insulting to the population to suggest that the group tearing apart everything they held most dear were 'nothing but cowards' since everybody knew that they were much more and, as a result, much more terrible than that.

Distantly, he heard the grandfather clock downstairs chime midnight. Zack stood up and walked over to the rain-streaked window, resolving to finish the speech later.

Before him, he saw the entire scope of The Inside, which was bathed in the bright, yellow glare of the moving security lights all around the building. He observed the rolling green hills; clear, blue pools; and, most prominent of all, the soft, golden sands.

His eyes travelled slowly across the landscape and came to rest on a looming, dark shape that ran along the horizon. A shiver of ice-cold blood ran down Zack's spine. It was The Outside. The barren and desolate place where the Freedom Fighters were based, as well as many of their unruly supporters. He bit his lip; things were looking bad enough already without the fact that the FF were heavily recruiting – so much so that their agents were now spilling over the border. He shuddered at the thought. The enemies' filtration was like a giant oil spill, spreading a dark shadow across the world and devouring everything in its path. It showed no mercy.

As he gazed out of the window at the hulking silhouette of enemy territory, it suddenly hit Zack just how much of a mess The Inside government were in and just how long, very like an oil spill, it would take to clear up.

TWO

'Morning!' Zack greeted the Brand family as brightly as possible as he opened the door and stepped over the threshold into their state-of-the-art kitchen diner. 'Sorry I'm late.'

'Hello, Zack,' smiled Rosa, Samuel's stunningly beautiful wife, who was sitting at the head of the large, mahogany kitchen table.

'Hi,' grinned Lucy, who was the family's only daughter and one of Zack's closest friends. 'All right?'

'Barely,' her friend replied wearily. He held out the freshly completed speech, now tied in a tight scroll, to Samuel. 'Here you are, sir.'

'Thank you,' answered the older man. He took the paper, looking relieved, and set it down on the marble worktop.

'When are you due on the TV?' Lucy asked her father curiously.

He looked apprehensive. 'Eleven.'

'We'll be watching!' she told him cheerfully, attempting to stop him feeling nervous. 'Won't we, Zack?'

'Yep!' Zack replied, adding grimly to himself, *along with the rest of the population, who'll probably be throwing everything within reach at the screen.* Clearing his throat, he announced that he had work to do. 'See you later' he told Lucy and then he left, gloomily anticipating the day ahead.

✗

'Mr Brand, will you tell us exactly how you plan to deal with the current crisis?' asked the interviewer.

Lucy bit her lip as she watched her father being grilled for information by Rory Miller, the news presenter interviewing him. Since the press conference given that morning, which had concluded in the reading of Zack's speech, it seemed as though Rory had been asking the same question over and over again for the past half an hour, just rephrasing it every so often: 'How is this situation being rectified?' or 'how are the current political exertions being dealt with?'

To make matters worse, Michael Chester, Samuel's most vocal political adversary, had also been invited to the consultation, and things were getting undeniably ugly.

Chester had now cut across Lucy's dad's stammered reply, declaring with obvious zest that not enough was being done by the current government to remedy the catastrophe, and that if it was beyond their abilities, then perhaps a new party needed to take control. With that,

Chester flashed his movie star grin at the camera, his shockingly white teeth glistening menacingly.

Sitting next to Lucy on the sofa, Zack cursed under his breath, an outraged expression on his face.

On the screen, Miller was trying and failing to keep the peace, as the two politicians' argument became still more intense.

'...I am merely pointing out that if the government cannot handle the situation—' sneered Chester.

'With all due respect, Mr Chester, my government are making a vast amount of progress—' countered Brand.

'I'm afraid that your idea of "a vast amount of progress" is very different to mine!'

'Gentlemen, gentlemen, please!' Rory was becoming more and more flustered. 'Be civil!'

Samuel and Michael, who had both made an aggressive movement towards each other, sank back into their chairs.

Miller sighed with relief. 'Well, then, shall we go on?'

*

The rest of the interview passed without any more major disagreements, but it was clear to everyone watching that both men hugely disliked each other. It was therefore no surprise to see that, when the discussion finally drew to a close, there was a look of great relief on Rory Miller's face.

With a sigh, Lucy grabbed the remote and switched off the television set. 'Thank God that's over!' she declared.

'Hey!' Rosa scolded, 'don't let your dad hear you saying stuff like that when he gets home; he'll be a nervous wreck already!' She sounded firm, but there was barely concealed agreement visible in her eyes.

THREE

'Honestly, Liam!' exclaimed Sherona Hamilton, glaring at her best friend, 'd'you *ever* stop talking about your stupid guitar? It's getting really annoying!'

'My guitar is my baby!' replied Liam passionately. 'You've just never had feelings like mine.'

'Yep, it's official; you've finally gone *totally* insane!' cried Bliss Cookson, another member of the group. 'It's a flashy hunk of wood, that's all; not a flamin' person.'

Liam was incandescent with rage. '*How dare you?*' he fumed.

The others burst out laughing at his expression.

'Will you please keep it down?' implored Nerrisia Simons, her dark eyes heavily shadowed. 'I've got a splitting headache. The baby was crying all night.'

'I can't imagine having a baby brother,' Lucy commented. 'It must be so weird!'

They turned the corner, and the impressive silhouette of their school building came into view.

'Here we go, another day of pointless servitude

awaits!' sighed Bliss, 'Zack's so lucky that he doesn't have to go!'

'Yeah, really lucky,' Lucy agreed sarcastically, 'he spends his days cooped up in an office, trying to persuade the population that The Outside is no real threat. Not an easy feat at the moment, and that's just for starters!'

Bliss rolled her eyes dramatically, but she did not pursue the subject.

'Hi, guys!' shouted Jake Highbridge – a tall, blond, good-looking boy – who was standing just inside the school gates waving at them.

'Hi,' Bliss called to him.

He walked over with a slight swagger. 'All right?'

Bliss nodded. 'Yeah, thanks. You?'

Jake shrugged. 'OK.' Turning to Lucy, he added, 'I saw your dad on the TV yesterday; that Chester bloke looked a right smarmy git!'

Lucy nodded. 'I know. Zack says Dad's rivals are all the same.'

Before they could talk any more, the school bell rang out across the playground, and they had to run as fast as they could to catch up with the throng of students moving across to the school building, with their school bags bouncing on their backs.

✄

Later that afternoon, while her monotonous maths teacher – Mr Rowler – rambled on about Pythagoras' theorem, Bliss drummed her fingers absent-mindedly on her desk, looking out of the window at the deserted grounds.

'Bliss? Answer my question, please,' came Mr Rowler's irritated voice.

'I dunno, sir. Sorry and all that,' she replied, smiling innocently up at him while the class roared with admiration-filled laughter.

Mr Rowler frowned. 'Very well, perhaps a detention after school will stimulate your brain a little?'

'Nah, I don't think so!'

The laughter was renewed at that, and the teacher looked furious.

He turned away. 'My classroom at three o'clock, please,' he told her coldly.

Bliss beamed at the back of his head. 'Right you are!'

As she turned to look back out of the window, she resolved not to turn up to the detention; they were a waste of time anyway.

Bang! Bang! Bang!

The class jumped at the sound of the three deafening gunshots that had cut cleanly through the air.

Liam, who was sitting in the row in front of Bliss, twisted round in his chair, the vexed expression on his face mirroring everyone else's. 'I wonder who it is this time?' he whispered miserably.

The students of The Inside had come to expect sinister activity such as this in their everyday lives, but it didn't make it any less disturbing.

Mr Rowler looked anxiously out of the window, his dark eyebrows almost knitted together, before pulling his gaze back to his class. He spoke sombrely. 'All right, everybody, where were we?'

✕

At lunchtime, Lucy, Bliss, Nerrisia, Sherona and Liam walked down to their favourite spot, sat on the grass under the oak tree, and started taking out their lunch. All the while, no one said a word to each other, lost in their own thoughts about what had happened in maths.

Liam chewed thoughtfully on his sandwich and looked around at the others; with a start, he saw Nerrisia was crying. 'Nerris, are you OK?' he asked, breaking the silence.

She bit her trembling lip and wiped her sleeve across her sparkling, brown eyes, tears catching on her long eyelashes. Shaking her head, she sniffed loudly and hugged her knees to her chest. 'It's horrible, the stuff that's going on around here,' she whispered. 'Innocent people are getting killed just for looking at one of those terrorists. It's just horrible!'

Sherona patted her arm gently, 'I know.'

Once again, they descended into silence.

FOUR

'The man shot dead at ten past eleven yesterday morning has been identified as nineteen-year-old Bradley Close, a history student studying at the University of The Inside who had been missing since Saturday morning. He had three bullet wounds to the chest; this is a common method of capital punishment used by the Freedom Fighters – a terrorist group of Outside origin. Bradley is rumoured to have "betrayed" the group in some way, as stated on a note found beside his body. Bradley's parents were unavailable for comment.' A picture of Bradley Close, smiling, round-faced and dimpled, appeared on the screen behind the sober-faced news reader.

Rowan Smith, Liam's mother, sighed heavily as she looked at it. 'The poor boy,' she muttered sadly, sitting down on the cream leather sofa in the Smith's living room, 'and his poor family.'

Her son just nodded, deep in thought. Elodie Close, Bradley's sister, was in his year at school, and they were well acquainted. He thought about how she must be feeling and his stomach twisted.

At that moment, Skye – Liam's eleven-year-old sister – came downstairs dressed in a fluffy, unicorn-embroidered dressing gown and matching slippers. 'What's going on?' she queried.

Liam looked dejected as he pointed at the screen.

Skye saw what was on it and her face crumpled. 'Oh,' she whispered, before hurrying out of the room.

'I'll go after her,' Rowan decided, and followed her.

Liam felt a sinking feeling in the pit of his stomach as he looked at the reporter, who'd now moved on to a story of an armed robbery of a petrol station that'd happened in the middle of the night. Thankfully, no one had been injured. *First bit of good news I've had since yesterday morning*, thought Liam with a wry smile.

FIVE

The following morning, Zack was again sitting at his desk. He was in the middle of a phone call to a woman who had telephoned with a complaint against the security – or, rather, the lack of it – provided by Samuel Brand and his council.

Lucy walked into his study, and, when she saw her friend's exasperated expression, she smirked and waved cheerfully. 'Morning, having fun?'

He mouthed 'shut up!' and continued talking into the phone, determinedly keeping his voice pleasant. 'I understand, madam, it is just that if you wish to pursue your argument—'

The lady on the phone had evidently interrupted him, for he stopped talking and rolled his eyes at Lucy, who was forced to clamp her hand over her mouth to stop the splutter of laughter bubbling up inside her from escaping.

'Yes, I'll be sure to mention it to him,' Zack assured his caller. 'Goodbye, Mrs Pollington.' Barely suppressing a sigh of relief, he was finally able to hang up.

'Yes, I'll be sure to mention it to him.' Lucy imitated his voice, making it sound overly pacifying, as though he had been talking to a fractious toddler.

'Shut it!' he snapped, glaring at her.

'Tetchy!' she replied, grinning. 'Someone's in a mood!'

'It's that stupid woman from up the road; she's driving me insane! It's all "I shall be back in touch if I find the situation is not improving" and "Be sure to mention this to Mr Brand; I wish to hear his own views on the subject without delay". Nosey so and so!'

She burst out laughing. 'I might've known!'

Her friend ran a hand through his jet-black hair and sighed in frustration. 'Sometimes, I wonder why I do this job!'

'If I had a pound for every time I heard you say that, I'd live in a Beverly Hills mansion and have one spare for visitors!'

The phone started ringing again, and Zack groaned. 'Wish me luck,' he muttered as he picked it up.

She smiled, waved joyfully at him and left.

Unnoticed by either of them, Samuel – who was sitting at his own desk and supposedly frowning over a lengthy memo – had looked up and been studying Lucy and Zack. As his daughter disappeared, Samuel continued to consider his clerk.

Why, he wondered, did Zack continue to work for him? The boy was outstandingly clever, hard-working and could no doubt do almost anything he wanted if he were to return to full-time education. It was no secret that he did not enjoy his work; on the contrary, he positively loathed it. So why did he do it?

The answer was a secret, which Zack had never told anybody. Nor, if he could help it, would he ever do so.

SIX

The sun had almost set, leaving ribbons of orange and dark pink streaked across the sky. It was beautiful.

Bliss, leaning heavily on her windowsill, stared out of the window at the idyllic scene, with a small smile playing at the edges of her mouth.

In the garden below the window, fourteen children were playing a game of seven-a-side football. They, along with Bliss and some others, lived at Sunnyside Children's Home.

Aaron Blake, a particularly tough boy who was one year older than Bliss, kicked the ball very hard. It shot into the air, before flying through the window and slamming into the back of the silver photo frame perched on the sill, just a little way away from where Bliss's folded arms were resting.

'BLOODY HELL!' she bellowed, 'WATCH IT!'

'Ooooh!' mocked Aaron, raising his eyebrows. 'Pass the ball back then, Cookson!'

'Come and get it!' she retorted, banging the window shut.

The photo was lying face down, and Bliss hurried to pick it up. The picture showed four people standing on a beach. There was a gaunt woman with long, blonde hair that was blowing all around her. She was next to a tall, dark, sharply featured man who had his arm around her shoulders. Between them, there was an ashen-faced young boy of ten. He had similar shoulder-length, black hair to the man, who was evidently his father. The final person in the picture was a fragile-looking little girl of five. She had flyaway hair, electric-blue eyes and was holding tightly to the woman's hand. Bliss.

She didn't know why she cared about it so much. It wasn't as though she liked any of those shown in it, nor did they feel anything for her but deepest hatred.

Bliss, her older brother Nick, their mother Salina and father Jordan had lived in The Outside longer than anybody else in history. Her father had been the sole founder of the Freedom Fighters terrorist group and, until he was killed in a battle with those from The Inside, he had been their leader. Upon the night of his death, Bliss – then seven – had trekked alone into The Inside and been found half dead the following morning by an Inside soldier. She had then been placed into the care system, and it was what she'd known ever since.

The FF's reaction to her "betrayal" had been catastrophic. Ever since the day she was discovered to be missing, Bliss had been accused of cowardice, and hunted by anyone and everyone the Freedom Fighters could persuade to join them. Bliss shuddered as she thought of her adversaries, who were likely to be plotting her death at that very moment.

She yawned and stretched; perhaps an early night was in order. After yanking her royal-blue curtains over the window pane, she changed into her pyjamas and got into bed. Her head buzzing with unpleasant thoughts, she stared at the ceiling until – at long, long last – she drifted into sleep.

SEVEN

The long-haired, hooded man sitting at the head of the table kept his predatory eyes fixed on the opposite wall; the twenty men and women to his left and right were staring up at him, looks of mingled fear and admiration etched across their faces.

Nobody spoke.

The room they were gathered in was dark and neglected – lit only with the feeble, flickering light of a candle in the centre of them all, the only light bulb hanging limply from the ceiling, having given out long ago. The man cleared his throat, and everyone else sat up a little straighter, waiting eagerly for their leader to speak.

When he obliged, his voice was harsh and impatient. '*Where is she?*'

There was no reply.

'Very well,' barked the man. 'We will have to begin without her.'

However, before he could continue talking, the door at the other end of the room was pushed open and a woman walked in. Everyone turned to watch her, even the leader of the group lowered his gaze a little to study the newcomer.

'Harper, you're late,' he told her, his voice lowering in icy displeasure.

'Forgive me, sir,' she replied, making a kind of half bow in his direction, 'I was delayed.'

'I can see that,' he said curtly. 'Why?'

'Research into the mole, sir, like you asked.'

'Mmm. In that case, you are forgiven. This time.'

There was an ominous pause, in which a young man three places to the leader's right looked from one to the other, holding his breath.

'Come here,' the first man commanded, and Harper hastened to obey, not sitting down like the others but coming to stand just behind him – the allotted position of his second in command.

With the gaze of his audience at last returned to him, the speaker started to address the wall again. 'Things are grave, my friends,' he whispered – his voice quietening still more, so that the others around him had to lean forwards in order to hear. 'Very grave indeed.'

Seemingly for dramatic effect, he waited before continuing. Exactly how long for, nobody knew. A second? An hour?

At last, he spoke. 'Word has it that one of our new recruits is a mole working for The Inside government.'

There was a collective gasp of horror from all those at the table, but the woman called Harper just nodded.

The man gestured to her before continuing. 'That is what Harper has been looking into.' He half glanced towards her, and his gaze was followed by all of those present.

Harper locked her gaze with his for half a second, but he quickly looked away before going on with his speech.

'If any of you receive a new member of your cell at any point during the next few weeks, watch them meticulously. Do not let them out of your sight for a second. Once the mole completes the training programme, they will be inconceivably dangerous, so watch them like hawks. Do I make myself clear?'

'Yes, sir,' came a solemn chorus of responses.

He nodded his approval. 'This meeting is over.'

At the last words of the speaker, everybody who was seated stood up and made to him the same bowing gesture Harper had made earlier. With that, they left.

✗

'Nick Cookson, I reckon you could give your dad a run for his money!' declared Delilah Harper as she and Nick, her best friend, opened the door to his poky hotel room. They were staying in one of The Outside's countless, grotty, anonymous dwelling places with the third member of their cell, Lucas Knight. He was known to them as Luke.

'Thanks,' replied Nick, a smile playing on his lips as he removed his hood, 'and sorry if I embarrassed you earlier.'

'Yeah, well, I was late.' She headed over to the grimy minibar and retrieved a rust-coloured can. 'Beer?' she asked, reaching for another one.

He nodded. 'Thanks.'

The door opened, and the man who'd been sitting three places away from Nick entered the room: Luke. He came over and clapped Nick on the back. 'Nice one!' he told him, with a thin-lipped smile.

'Thanks,' repeated Nick. His black mobile started to ring, and he turned away. 'Hello?' he snapped into it. His frown deepened, and he began to pace up and down the room, watched continuously by Luke and Delilah.

'I see,' he said, his dark eyebrows virtually knitted together now. 'I see. Two? Very well!' He ended the call looking savage.

'What—' Luke began, but his words were halted in their tracks.

'BLOODY HELL!' roared Nick, lion-like, as he threw the phone away. It hit the wall with a powerful thud. 'Two,' he muttered, more to himself than either of the others. 'Two!'

'Two what?' ventured Delilah, blinking at him.

'New recruits,' he explained. 'That was the training camp. Two people have just finished the course – Paul Broke and Layna Johns; they're on their way over now.'

When neither Luke nor Delilah reacted to these words, Nick rolled his eyes and elucidated, his features darkening with every word. 'There are two new recruits in our cell alone,' he explained. 'How the hell are we going to weed out a mole in the whole of the FF complex if new recruits keep arriving like this?'

A look of awful realisation appeared on the others' faces, and Delilah swore badly.

There was a knock at the door, and Nick was instantly alert. He signalled to them to remain quiet and walked silently over to the door. 'Password?' he breathed through the keyhole.

'Inside irreverence,' replied the person on the other side.

Satisfied, Nick put a hand out to unlock it and three people – two men and a teenage girl – entered.

The tallest of the men looked from Nick to Delilah to Luke. 'Who's in charge?' he asked bluntly.

'That'd be me,' Nick answered, looking and sounding distinctly irritated.

The man held out a rough hand. 'Jerry Mistral – Commander of the training camp.'

As Nick reluctantly shook hands, he said, with a twisted smile, 'Nicholas Cookson – leader of the FF.'

The younger man and the girl, who were obviously Johns and Broke, looked awed.

After a brief pause, Nick gestured to Luke and Delilah. 'The rest of my cell: Lieutenant Delilah Harper and Corporal Lucas Knight.'

Jerry nodded at them. 'Evening to both of you.'

'Evening,' muttered Luke, his eyes fixed on Layna, a lecherous grin on his face.

Layna didn't smile back. Her gaze was resting on Nick, the admiration still visible in her midnight-blue eyes.

'Come in then, quickly,' Nick ordered her and Paul.

They looked at Jerry, who made shooing gestures at them. Glancing apprehensively at one another, they hurried inside.

Without another word, Nick shut the door.

'Sir!' Paul gasped, 'I can't tell you… the honour—'

'Shut it,' interjected Nick.

The harsh interruption seemed to hit Paul in the stomach, and his mouth closed like a steel trap. An embarrassed expression now clouded his face and a half-concealed look of annoyance flashed into his eyes. 'I'm sorry, sir.'

'I said shut it,' hissed the terrorists' leader. 'Both of you, listen to me.' His stare rested on first Paul and then Layna. 'You two need to know something. Neither of you are trusted by myself or my colleagues, not until you've proven your worth.'

This statement hung in the air around them, and colour jumped into both the new arrivals' cheeks.

'Luke,' Nick continued sharply, 'show them the ropes.'

At these words, Luke looked jubilant; his gaze moved to Layna and he smiled. 'Good idea.'

'Delilah, I need to speak to you, in private,' Nick went on.

Much to her indignation, he pulled her into the small, tiled bathroom and locked the door.

'Why *here*?' she asked, looking around resentfully.

'Sorry,' he apologised, 'but this is important.'

She raised her eyebrows and gave him a sceptical look. 'Important enough to drag me into this place?'

'I need you to get to know them,' he explained, with a glance at the door, 'as quickly as you can. I need to know anything and everything you can tell me. First rule in this life: know your enemy.'

She nodded. 'OK. Now can we please get out of here? Being in a bathroom with *you* is not my idea of fun!'

He grinned. 'You and me both!'

They both started laughing.

EIGHT

'What's the name of this girl again?' Zack asked Samuel as they drove along in his sleek, silver sports car towards the top-secret location in which they were meeting the mole within the FF for the first time.

'Layna Johns,' he replied. 'Funny kid, apparently.'

'Mmm, right.' Zack nodded briefly, looking out of the window as they passed some green fields.

They continued their journey in silence until they reached their destination. Here, they climbed out. Both, though they did not voice their feelings, were exceptionally nervous.

The pair of them arrived at a white-painted door, and Samuel knocked three times.

A serious-looking man opened it, and, upon seeing who was on the threshold, he smiled briefly and shook their hands. 'My name's Robert Ferguson, come in,' he told them.

Doing as they were asked, they looked around.

The room was small and stuffy, but there was a freshly varnished, rectangular table crammed into it – at which sat another man, who was wearing a grey suit.

With some difficulty, given his bulk, the man got to his feet and hurried over. 'Mr Brand!' he boomed, 'Mr McGregor!' He grasped each of their hands in turn and shook them.

'H-hello,' stammered Zack, surprised at the recognition of his name. 'Nice to meet you.'

'The pleasure's all mine, lad, all mine!'

'Really, Acer,' scolded Ferguson, 'the poor boy doesn't even know who you are; he's not used to your jovial ways.'

The man named Acer gave a hearty laugh. 'You are quite right. How inane of me!' He turned to Zack and said, at even greater volume, 'I'm Julian Acer.'

Zack smiled but said nothing. It was hard to know how to respond, his own introduction already over.

There was another round of handshaking, and then Samuel spoke. 'Gentlemen, where is Miss Johns?'

'She'll be here in a moment,' replied Ferguson confidently. 'It will be difficult for her to get away from the others in her cell.'

Samuel nodded. 'Of course.'

There was a pause in which Acer twiddled his wiry moustache, and Zack looked towards the door, waiting curiously for Layna to enter.

Obligingly, less than a minute later, the door was opened and someone stepped into the room.

His heart skipped a beat. She was beautiful, with glossy, golden waves of hair that dangled down her back, and skin that looked soft and flawless. Then there were her eyes. *Oh God, her eyes...*

'Layna!' exclaimed Ferguson, bringing Zack back to earth with a bump.

Zack blinked, and Samuel grinned at him, seeming to read his thoughts as Robert pulled Layna further into the room towards them.

'Layna Johns, meet Samuel Brand, Zackary McGregor and Julian Acer.'

On the last name, Layna relaxed slightly. 'We've met,' she smiled.

Acer nodded. 'I found her,' he told the room at large, puffing out his chest haughtily, and reminding Layna irresistibly of a swaggering peacock.

'Found her indeed!' scoffed Ferguson. 'You just realised her potential, that is all.'

Layna blushed scarlet, and Zack took it upon himself to come to her rescue.

'Shall we… um…' he began, but Layna had turned her face fully towards him and he stammered into silence, apparently dumbstruck.

'Good idea,' smiled Samuel, his eyes flickering between the pair of teenagers.

Zack's face, too, was crimson, and he looked determinedly at the floor.

Robert and Julian didn't seem to notice anything strange, and they led the way back to the table. Layna, Zack and Samuel joined them.

The atmosphere in the room changed at once. The very air around them seemed to ooze tension suddenly.

Ferguson was looking distinctly grim as he spoke. 'We all know why we are here, I take it? The purpose of this meeting is to address the inexpressibly courageous decision Miss Johns has made to serve The Inside government as an ally within the Freedom Fighters organisation.'

Layna stared steadily back at the many faces now turned in her direction, but Zack noticed her shuffle down slightly in her chair and he smiled at her encouragingly. She returned his smile gratefully.

'Miss Johns,' Samuel began, his eyes meeting hers, 'I must impress upon you the seriousness of what you have chosen to do...' He paused. 'And offer you a final chance to change your mind.'

'No,' Layna told him firmly, 'I want to go through with it.'

'Layna, I beg of you, listen to me. If you do this, you will be in constant danger – you may even be killed,' Samuel stated. There was no beating about the bush, no stretching the truth, just cold, hard facts.

'I know,' she whispered, biting her lip.

'You're so brave.' The words were out of Zack's mouth before he could stop them, and he groaned inwardly with embarrassment.

She looked right at him, her eyes warm as a summer's day. 'Thanks,' she murmured.

They looked away from each other, feeling hugely awkward.

While the others talked, Zack could not take any interest in what was going on around him. Suddenly, in the space of just a few minutes, his head seemed to have become capable only of thinking of Layna. Every time he looked at her, he felt an odd, indefinable swooping sensation in the pit of his stomach, as though he could soar over the highest mountain imaginable without a second thought. It was a wonderful feeling.

'So, it's decided,' declared Julian, standing up at last. 'You, Layna, will try to report to Samuel and Zack at least once a month – although, of course, this may not always be possible, given your situation.'

She nodded distractedly. 'Yes, yes, of course.' As she spoke, her eyes remained fixed on Zack.

With that, the others in the room followed Julian's lead and surged towards the doorway, leaving only Zack lagging behind.

'Zack! *Zack!*'

He whirled round to see that Layna had broken away from the others and was coming towards him. It was she who had called his name. Again, the peculiar feeling in his stomach occurred, making him strangely nervous.

'Er… hi,' Layna mumbled, not quite meeting his gaze.

'Hi,' Zack croaked.

'I… I just wanted to thank you again, for what you said back there.'

'That? Oh, it was nothing,' he told her, though he felt delighted with her praise. 'It was the truth.'

'It was really nice of you,' she told him softly and – quite unexpectedly – she kissed him on the cheek.

Zack's stomach did an elated loop the loop.

'Well,' Layna smiled, 'I'll be seeing you, I guess.' Blushing slightly, she hovered for a moment, unsure what to say or do. Searching Zack's face for guidance, she saw with relief that he was just as new to this as she was. 'Sooner rather than later, I hope.'

'Yeah,' he muttered, slightly stunned. 'See you.'

She nodded. 'Soon,' and with a last thankful wave, she walked away.

NINE

'I just don't get what you see in her,' Bliss asserted to Zack as they sat in a café with the others. 'I mean she's pretty and everything, but do you ever spend more than ten minutes together?'

'Of course we do!' he objected, then – hesitating – he added, 'we're both just busy with work.'

'Yeah, newsflash – you're sixteen! That excuse only comes into play when you're at least twenty-five,' Bliss retorted.

Sherona nodded. 'Definitely!'

'Why don't you take tonight off?' Lucy suggested. 'Dad's not got any speeches due for ages; I'm sure he can survive without you for one night.'

'Yeah,' encouraged Nerrisia, 'go to a restaurant or something.'

It was just shy of a month since Zack and Layna's first meeting, and they'd been seeing each other for a fortnight and a half. Despite what the others believed, they spent every possible moment together.

'OK, I'll ask her,' he decided at last, pulling out his mobile. After a while, he spoke into it. 'Hey, baby, how're you?'

He stood up and left the café to continue his call outside, leaving the others to shamelessly discuss the future of his love life.

'Two weeks tops' predicted Liam, 'and that's if they're really lucky'

Bliss nodded. 'She's not right for him.'

'Total opposites,' Lucy agreed.

'Yeah, they've got no chance,' declared Sherona knowledgeably.

Nerrisia was looking out of the window at her friend, who was now engrossed in his phone call and smiling broadly. She had never seen him so happy. 'I think,' she mused, 'they've got every chance in the world.'

'Soppy weirdo,' muttered Bliss, but she started to grin too.

⚡

'So, how are things with the FF?' Zack asked Layna as they scanned their menus while sitting at their table in Cherry Trees, her favourite restaurant.

She sighed. 'Can we talk about something else for a change?'

He mentally kicked himself. Why did he always have to bore her like this? 'Sorry,' he apologised, 'I just—'

'Care about me,' she supplied, laughing, 'I know.'

He looked embarrassed. 'Sorry,' he repeated.

'Forget it,' she told him, leaning forwards, her menu closed and discarded.

'OK,' he breathed, making an identical movement towards her.

As they kissed, an elderly couple glanced disapprovingly at them, both muttering things about 'the youth of today' and 'disgusting habits'.

They ignored them, completely lost in the bliss of it all.

Eventually, Zack pulled away, beaming. 'All forgotten.'

The old man tutted, his wife shook her head, and the young, blond waiter standing a few metres away looked self-conscious, but neither Zack nor Layna cared about any of them; they merely gazed at each other, their eyes bright with sheer happiness.

Zack beckoned to the waiter, still grinning cheerfully. 'Excuse me, would you take our order, please?'

The waiter swallowed. 'Y-yes, of course,' he replied, still looking slightly uncomfortable as he hurried over to them, his pen poised above his notepad.

They each gave their order, and the waiter wrote down what they wanted and turned away.

Zack watched him go before turning back to Layna. 'I love you,' he whispered.

TEN

'I don't get why we have to leave,' Paul Broke complained loudly to Luke as they packed their clothes into an ancient brown rucksack. 'I mean, what's the point?'

The icy reply he received did not come from Luke's direction. 'The point, you pathetic git, is so we don't get found by Insiders and have our throats slit in the process!'

Paul spun round to find Nick glowering at him from the doorway. 'S-sir! I thought—'

'Thought I couldn't hear?' Nick snarled. 'Thought, while I wasn't in the same room as you, you'd have a bloody good dig at my strategic movements? Thought that you – a good-for-nothing, first-time recruit, already under intense suspicion – would go around boasting about *how much you could better my leadership skills?*' Suddenly, without warning, Cookson leapt across the room and clasped his hands around Broke's throat, pinning him against the wall. 'Don't you contradict me – to my face or behind my back – ever again. Do you understand?'

Paul spluttered and rasped but did not speak; his eyes were wide with pure terror.

'I SAID, DO YOU UNDERSTAND?' bellowed Nick, tightening his grip regardless of Paul's desperate attempts to free himself. 'DO YOU?'

'Yes!' Paul croaked. 'Yes!'

Nick let go of him, and Paul sighed with relief; however, his jubilation was short-lived.

'Luke,' Nick hissed, 'kill him.'

Tears were running down Paul's face. 'No! Forgive me, please! My wife, my children. *Pleeease!*'

Ignoring these protests, Luke put a hand in his jacket pocket and pulled out a pistol, turning it over and over in his fingers, stroking it lovingly.

'Do it!' snapped his superior. 'Now!'

Almost automatically, Knight raised the gun and pulled the trigger. The bang that issued from the weapon was accompanied by Paul Broke's final, terrified, bloodcurdling scream.

Delilah and Layna appeared in the doorway, with their own rucksacks already full and on their backs.

'What the—' Delilah began.

Nick held up a hand to stop her. 'We have to leave immediately.' Without so much as a waver in his voice or a flicker of expression, he gestured to the lifeless form of Paul – sprawled on the floor and bathed in a pool of dark-red blood. 'Once the authorities find this, they'll know we were here; we need to be long gone before then.'

Layna's face was pale with shock, but when she spoke it was with a steadfast pretence of awe and triumph. 'Is… is that it then, sir? Has the mole been neutralised?'

Nick put his head on one side, considering. 'No. I don't think so.'

A small gasp escaped Layna's dry lips, and her eyes suddenly seem glued to the corpse, at which she had not looked since it had fallen. 'Then why, sir? Why did you have to kill him?'

'He was a liability,' Nick replied simply. 'First lesson, Private Johns – I will not stand for weak links in my chain of command.' With that, he walked away.

ELEVEN

She was running for her life.

As she rounded the corner, a figure dropped into her path from the roof of a derelict estate building. 'Hello, beautiful,' he leered. 'Tried to give me the slip, did you? Well, I'd better teach you a lesson, hadn't I?' He pulled her towards him and lifted her chin – the gesture a grotesque parody of the first kiss she would not now live to receive. Smiling, he used his free hand to withdraw a bloodstained, silver knife from his pocket.

'No!' cried the child. 'Don't! I'll do anything, just don't hurt me!' She looked pleadingly at him. 'I… I'm only sixteen. I… I didn't know what Brad was doing; I didn't support… NO!'

Before another thought could enter the terrified brain of his victim, the man surged forwards and slid the knife easily between her ribs.

With a final, childish whimper, Elodie Close crumpled like a broken doll.

Lucas Knight stared down at his handiwork with satisfaction for a moment, letting the blood gush over his gloved hands before bending to retrieve his blade. It wasn't the biggest coup he'd ever pulled off – but there really was something incredibly gratifying about a job well done. He polished the knife idly with the cuffs of his jacket and strode silently away from the devastation, careful not to rush unnecessarily.

Freedom Fighter survival law number one: haste means suspicion; caution means innocence.

⚡

'Well?' Nick demanded as Luke re-entered the motel room. 'Did you do it?'

'Signed, sealed and delivered,' replied Knight with a callous grin. 'Very neatly done. Not too much blood.'

'Excellent! Now on to bigger and better things!'

'The parents?' asked Delilah.

'The parents,' Nick confirmed, nodding. He turned to Layna, who was studying a blueprint of the Houses of Parliament and selecting appropriate entrances from which to infiltrate the building. 'Johns, they're your responsibility.'

She looked up. 'Yes, sir.'

'You have three hours. If the deed isn't done by then, there will be severe consequences,' Nick continued.

'Yes, sir.'

He came closer. 'Get to work,' he said, before gesturing to the blueprint. 'Leave that with me.'

She nodded and stood up. 'You got weapons?'

'Naturally, in the cupboard.' Nick jerked his head backwards, indicating the dilapidated bathroom behind them.

'Right.' Layna hurried into the bathroom and opened the white cabinet on the wall. Five different pistols and at least a dozen knives were stored there. All were deadly. Disgusted with herself, she picked up a shining dagger and placed it inside her jacket, not intending to use it.

Reappearing, she plastered a carefree smile on her face. 'No time like the present.'

Nick nodded his approval, pleasantly surprised by the new girl's willingness to perform. 'I like your thinking, Layna.'

'Thank you, sir.'

'Off you go. You still have to prove to me you're not soft.'

'Yes, sir.' Layna wanted nothing more than to get out of there and call for assistance to rescue Mr and Mrs Close, but she was careful not to show it.

As she left, she heard Delilah mutter something almost unintelligible under her breath. 'Good luck; you'll need it.'

TWELVE

'How are they?' Layna asked Samuel an hour and a half later, as they stood in the lobby of The Inside police station with Lucy, Zack and the others.

'Shaken, obviously, but otherwise OK,' Samuel answered flatly.

'Could've been a lot worse, I reckon,' Liam put in, 'if you hadn't been appointed as their assassin.'

The thought of this made them all feel as if their stomachs had plunged down a lift shaft. A ripple of anxiety passed around the group.

'So what's going to happen now?' asked Nerrisia, changing the subject quickly. 'Where will Mr and Mrs Close go? Not back to the house, I suppose?'

Samuel shook his head and elaborated. 'We have a top-secret safe house ready for them. Far away from here.'

'They must feel dreadful,' Lucy sighed. 'Their son's dead, their daughter's dead and now this.'

'I know,' agreed Sherona, 'I feel so bad for them. Why do things like this always happen here?'

Nobody answered.

After several minutes of uncomfortable silence, Police Constable Laura Timmons, the police officer in charge of the protection of Mr and Mrs Close, approached them.

'Excuse me,' she said briskly, 'is one of you Layna Johns?'

'Yeah, that's me,' Layna told her, confused.

Laura regarded her. 'Mr and Mrs Close want to speak with you.'

'What about?' demanded Zack, instantly protective. 'She's not done anything wrong.'

Irritated, the officer turned to him. 'I hardly think it's any of your business.'

'PC Timmons,' Samuel interrupted, frowning, 'I'll thank you not to talk to my employee like that.'

She looked around and gave a start. 'Mr Brand, sir! Forgive me; I didn't recognise you!'

Samuel nodded curtly before glancing at Zack. 'I think Layna ought to do what she's asked.'

'But...'

Before Zack could finish, Laura pounced on Samuel's words. 'Good! Come with me, Layna.'

With a fleeting apologetic look at her boyfriend, Layna nodded and followed the police officer out of the room.

The two of them soon arrived at PC Timmons's office, opened the door and entered. The room was smallish, but pleasant; it had an oak desk and chair, and a two-seater leather sofa, upon which Mr and Mrs Close were sat.

'Hello,' Layna greeted the occupants of the room.

'Hello,' replied Mr Close sombrely; unsmiling as he squeezed his wife's shoulders.

'You saved us,' Mrs Close breathed, her voice shaking. 'You saved our lives.'

'I—' stammered Layna uncertainly.

'Our children. Why not our children?' cut in Mrs Close.

Layna swallowed, feeling suddenly as if she had walked into some sort of trap. 'I'm sorry? I don't quite understand.'

'Our children are dead, and it's all *your* fault,' spat Mrs Close, her eyes suddenly narrowed. 'You should have protected them; you should have stopped those murderous terrorists from slaughtering our children!'

Before anyone else could react, Mrs Close had leapt to her feet, scratching and tearing at Layna's face, screaming insults at the top of her voice as red gashes appeared all over Layna's skin.

'Mrs Close, calm down!' ordered PC Timmons, forcing her way in between them, her expression shocked.

'Sweetheart, stop this,' Mr Close pleaded, standing up and helping to pull his wife and Layna apart. 'She did her best.'

Mrs Close struggled against her husband's grip, sobbing and quaking. 'She killed them, Bryan! She *killed* them!'

The desperate sound of her voice rent the air, and Layna felt a mixture of pity, fear and shock.

'Layna, perhaps you should leave,' advised Laura sharply. 'I think I ought to stay and deal with the situation.'

Layna didn't need telling twice. She pelted back towards the others, not stopping until she'd flung herself into Zack's arms, sobbing.

'What happened?' he asked, looking concerned and taken aback. 'God, look at your face!'

'Mrs Close!' Layna wept, 'She... she...'

'*She* did this to you – after you saved her life?' gasped Nerrisia. 'That's awful!'

With a tearful hiccough, Layna explained what had happened in PC Timmons's office, much to the outrage of those around her.

Liam frowned. 'Just when you think you've done something right, eh?'

'Yeah,' agreed Sherona. 'It's typical, isn't it? You think you're safe and then... bam!'

'Mmm,' nodded Samuel. 'I have to admit; you might be right about that.' He sighed. 'Maybe Chester was on to something when he said a new government should be in charge.'

'Dad! Don't talk like that!' Lucy protested, 'Chester's a stupid prat; he's got no idea what he's on about.'

'Right,' Zack agreed. He had taken Layna over to the waiting-room sofa, and they were sitting down on it, holding hands.

'Hmm, I dare say that is a matter of opinion,' replied Samuel, looking thoroughly unconvinced.

There was silence for a moment while everybody digested fully what had happened.

'We should get you to hospital,' Bliss told Layna eventually.

'No,' she replied at once, 'I can't. I've already been gone way too long; if I stay out any longer, my cell will just get even more suspicious.'

'She's right,' Samuel agreed heavily. 'It'd be too dangerous for her to be away much longer.'

They all filed out of the station, and then Zack kissed Layna goodbye.

'Call me later, OK?' he murmured.

'I'll try,' she told him. 'See you soon.'

'Yeah.'

The pair of them kissed again, more passionately.

Bliss tapped her friend on the shoulder. 'Hello? Still here, you know!'

Pulling away, Zack grinned. 'So?'

Bliss made a swipe at him.

He dodged and then laughed. 'OK, OK!'

Bliss rolled her eyes dramatically. 'Thank you!'

Lucy pulled a face. 'What's happened to you, Zack? You never used to be this gross. Weird, yeah, but never like *this*!'

Samuel laughed, 'It'll happen to you one day.'

'Yeah, well, it's still gross!' muttered his daughter mutinously.

'I'll second that,' agreed Sherona, grinning.

'And me!' Liam chimed in.

Layna sighed; they didn't understand. When she was with Zack, it was like nothing she'd ever felt before; all of a sudden it seemed to her that, as long as she had him by her side, nothing else mattered. 'I really have to go,' she told the others. 'See you.'

As she walked away, Layna's mobile vibrated; 'Luke calling' flashed briefly onto the screen. She bit her lip. *Now for the tricky bit.*

THIRTEEN

'What took you so long?' barked Nick as soon as Layna opened the door of the hotel room and stepped inside.

'Sorry, they put up a fight.' Gesturing to the scratches on her face, she sat down on the end of Luke's bed.

'But you did finish the job, didn't you?' Nick asked, a hint of danger in his voice. 'I mean, your targets, they *are* dead?'

'Yes, sir,' replied Layna, 'of course.'

'You disposed of the bodies, I trust?'

'Yes, sir.'

He smiled silkily. 'You do realise, Layna, that this leaves us with no proof that what you say is true.'

Slightly panicked but careful not to show it, she looked him straight in the eye. 'When Paul and I were at training camp, we were taught to destroy evidence of murder.'

Luke and Delilah looked at her in surprise. New recruits had passed through the cell before and none of them had dared take that tone with Nick until they'd served opposite him for at least a year.

'She's got a point,' Delilah muttered. 'Face it, Nick, she passed your test.'

Nick grunted but said nothing. They were right – and he knew it.

Instead, Delilah was the one to speak once more. 'Beer?' she asked her colleagues as she strolled over to the grimy minibar in the corner.

Luke and Nick both nodded, but Layna shook her head. 'I don't like it,' she replied.

Delilah raised her eyebrows as she fetched the drinks. 'Right.'

'I've never heard an FF member say that before,' Luke grinned. 'I like a girl who's different.'

Layna merely shrugged her shoulders, and a flash of annoyance crossed Luke's face as he took his can from Delilah and sipped at it.

'What're you planning to do next then?' he asked gruffly, looking at Nick.

'We've stamped out four traitors, now onto another.' Nick's tone of flat indifference did not waver, but a ripple of interest passed between the others as he spoke.

'The mole?' Luke asked, the tip of his tongue flickering in a serpentine movement across his top lip while a brief, violent flash of excitement appeared on his face.

Nick did not make eye-contact with him, instead staring fixedly at the opposite wall as he spoke. 'Yep.'

If the other members of her cell hadn't been so single-mindedly focused on their drinks, they would have noticed that Layna had stiffened suddenly, digging her nails into her palms and biting her lip nervously.

FOURTEEN

The following evening, Liam, Sherona, Zack, Lucy, Nerrisia and Bliss were sitting on tatty, old beanbags in Liam's attic. They were poring over a pile of handwritten song lyrics, chewing the ends of their pencils and sharing the contents of a bag of jellybeans that was lying between them.

'I don't know,' Sherona sighed, taking her pencil out of her mouth and reaching for the sheet of paper on the top of the pile. 'This bit doesn't really make sense.' She pointed at a line towards the bottom of the page; the others leaned in to look.

Lucy sung the line to herself, 'If despair is another rain cloud, then love is you and me.' She nodded. 'Yeah, I see what you mean.'

Liam clicked his tongue in thought for a moment. 'How about "If despair is a *dark grey* rain cloud"? That sounds better, doesn't it?'

'Yeah, it's great!' Bliss enthused, picking up a jelly bean.

The six friends were spending Zack's night off working on songs for their amateur band Wild Ones and, slowly but surely, they were making progress.

'Right, we're all done,' Zack declared, smiling. 'The gig on Friday should be awesome.'

Nerrisia looked around the room, feeling pleased with their nights' work. Three new songs had been written, four melodies had been composed, and they'd got through three bags of sweets between them. It'd been a good night.

Stifling a yawn, Bliss stood up. 'I'd better get back,' she told them, looking slightly gloomy. 'See ya.'

'Already?' asked Liam. 'It's only just nine o'clock.'

'I know,' she sighed. 'It's Sunnyside's stupid curfew.'

Sherona grimaced. 'Poor you!'

Rolling her eyes, Bliss nodded, 'I know.' She put on a false whimper. 'Poor, sweet, little me! Get the violins out, everyone!'

They burst into laughter, and Lucy flicked a jelly bean at her.

Bliss dodged and grinned. 'Bye!'

'Bye,' the others chorused as she left.

Liam yawned loudly and leaned back on his beanbag. 'I feel sorry for her sometimes,' he mused, looking at the door Bliss had just closed, with a sympathetic expression on his face, 'living in that stupid kids' home.'

Nerrisia tutted and nodded. 'Mmm.'

Sherona shook her head. 'Nah. She's tough; she's not the type to mope around feeling sorry for herself.'

'Yeah,' Liam conceded, 'but even so…'

'Hey, guys!' Lucy laughed, pulling a face. 'No need to be the voices of doom and gloom!'

'Sorry' they chorused.

Zack's mobile alerted him to a text message. It was from Layna:

Hi, just wanted 2 let u know I'm OK. Don't call back. Being watched. Luv u xxx

He swallowed. Thinking of her alone with three terrorists made his stomach turn, but at least he knew she was all right. 'Love you too,' he whispered, closing the phone.

FIFTEEN

'Hi, Liam!'

With a sigh, Liam looked up to see Rebecca Bamforth – a particularly annoying girl from his class – making her way over to him, fluttering her long eyelashes. 'Hi,' he muttered, glaring at the others, who were already struggling to hold back their laughter.

Whenever she spied him in the playground, Rebecca would pounce on Liam like a lioness, taking every opportunity to shamelessly flirt with him.

'Rebecca, I'm kind of busy right—' he started to say, knowing before a single word had left his mouth that resistance was futile.

'I was just wondering if you're, like, still up for helping me with my maths homework tonight?' She smiled like a Barbie doll and giggled girlishly. 'I'm *reeeeally* looking forward to it!' She watched him expectantly, bouncing up and down on the balls of her feet, giving the impression of an over-excited toddler.

Bliss elbowed him, and he jumped.

'I… er… sure,' he stammered, embarrassed.

'Great!' Rebecca winked and sat down next to him. 'Thanks.'

'No… no worries.' He shuffled away from her, trying to keep smiling, while the others exchanged looks.

'I wouldn't ask,' Rebecca ploughed on, edging after him and laying a hand on his shoulder. 'It's just, I've always been terrible at maths, and you're, like, Pisces or something!'

'You mean Pythagoras,' Lucy muttered darkly, glowering at Rebecca and hunching over angrily. 'Any fool knows that!'

Rebecca whimpered and stood up, sticking her nose into the air. 'Whatever. See you later, Li Li.'

As she marched away, Liam's friends turned to stare at him.

'You're opting to spend the evening with *her*?' asked Sherona incredulously. 'Seriously?'

'Never mind that!' Bliss interrupted, grinning. 'Did she just call you *Li Li*?'

Liam went scarlet, while Nerrisia and Sherona fell about laughing.

Lucy was still scowling in the direction Rebecca had gone, her face thunderous. 'That complete cow!' she exclaimed furiously.

'Ooooh,' Bliss mocked, pulling a soppy face.

'Oh shut up!' Lucy leapt to her feet, 'I'm going to the cafeteria!'

Liam frowned. 'What's up?'

Lucy said nothing, just stalked away, bristling with anger and indignation.

'What's got into her?' Liam asked, perplexed.

Nerrisia sighed. 'Isn't it obvious?'

When Liam shrugged, she rolled her eyes and gave up on him. In his own, slow time, he'd realise what was going on. *At least,* she thought to herself, *I hope so.*

✦

Back at Lucy's house, Zack was tapping his fingers against his desk, impatiently waiting for Mrs Pollington's associate to phone him back.

Mrs Pollington had been sticking her nose in yet again and, this time, she'd recruited the help of her fellow displeased members of the public. Now Zack was being bombarded with threats and complaints.

Prudence Rose was one of the most prominent of these letter writers, and, after three weeks of messages, Zack had finally decided to telephone the landline number she had listed and demand to hear the reasons for her behaviour. So far, he had been unsuccessful in reaching her.

Sighing heavily, he wondered for the thousandth time what it would be like to go to school with the others. For a moment, he pictured himself giving up his job and re-joining Inside High, but he quickly pushed the thought away, thinking of his secret. He mustn't let himself be tempted to give up his job; the money was needed far too much for that. He shook his head firmly and picked up the receiver, deciding to try Mrs Rose again.

However, to his great surprise, he found himself dialling Layna's mobile. When she didn't answer, he assumed she must be busy with the FF activities and rang off without leaving a message.

Right at that moment, he felt very, very alone.

SIXTEEN

Layna knocked on Samuel Brand's door, eager to tell him her most recent findings. However, it was Zack who answered the door.

'Hello, you!' he smiled when he saw who it was.

She gave him a quick kiss before stepping over the threshold. 'Hi.'

'Sir!' Zack yelled into the house, 'Layna's here!'

After a brief pause, Samuel made his way into the hallway. 'Hello, Layna,' he greeted her.

She nodded politely at him. 'Samuel.'

'You sounded very keen on the phone; I take it this is not a social call?' Samuel enquired.

'No, sir.'

'I see. Shall we go through to my office? Feel free to come too, Zack.'

They followed him into the room and sat down.

Samuel looked at Layna and asked, 'may I get you a drink?'

'No, thank you.'

'Very well. Let's get straight to the point then. What is it you wanted to tell me?'

Leaning forwards, Layna began to explain. 'There's to be a meeting of every FF agent and the FF Commander a week tomorrow.'

Looking interested, Samuel nodded at her encouragingly. 'Will you be there?'

She nodded. 'Yes.'

'And what is this meeting about?' Samuel pressed; his fingers knotted together as he studied her expectantly.

'There are plans to assassinate several MPs over the next couple of weeks. I think the meeting might be something to do with that.'

'Can't you be sure?' asked Samuel, a slight frown crossing his face, 'I mean, if you're invited to this meeting, surely you should know more about it?'

Layna shook her head. 'Sorry, but the Commander is very secretive, he only confides the exact details of his plans to his lieutenant.'

'I see. Does this man, the Commander, have a name?'

'Yeah, of course,' Layna replied, then she hesitated, 'but if you don't mind, I'd like to keep it to myself for a while longer. If I can have a bit more time to get to know him before I give you his details and the police go in to arrest him, the information I can give you would help us to understand the way the FF works better, as opposed to just arresting one commander.'

Zack nodded. 'She's right.'

Samuel considered them for a moment. 'All right,' he conceded at last, 'on your heads be it.'

'Thank you, sir' Layna replied, smiling.

They talked for half an hour, discussing the meeting and what was to be done if Layna's suspicions were correct.

After this, Samuel got to his feet. 'Right,' he announced, 'that'll be all.'

Layna nodded and both she and Zack rose to their feet. 'OK.'

As they left the room and headed down the hallway, Zack caught Layna's arm and pulled her into a corner. 'Thanks for the information,' he told her. 'It's really useful.'

She shrugged. 'It's my job, isn't it?'

He nodded. 'I guess. Look, be careful, won't you? I don't think I could bear it if anything happened to you out there. I love you.' He said all this very quickly, as though he was embarrassed to admit his fears.

Blushing violently, he opened his mouth to say something apologetic, but she stopped him by leaning forwards and gently kissing him on the lips.

'I know,' she whispered as they broke apart, 'I love you too.' She squeezed his hand briefly. 'Don't worry about me.'

In the pocket of her jeans, her phone started to ring, alerting them both to the fact that her cell must have noticed her lengthy absence.

'I'd better go,' she sighed, looking regretful.

'Yeah,' he agreed heavily.

Together, they walked to the end of the drive.

'See you,' Layna told him as she walked away.

Zack turned to go back into the house, thinking of what life must be like with the FF – surrounded by murderous terrorists. He shuddered; it must be horrible. *Hang on in there, babes,* he thought.

SEVENTEEN

'Wafer, if there is something you would like to say, you will share it with the rest of us!' Nick demanded, glaring down at Oliver Wafer, who jumped at the sound of his name being called and flinched under the severity of the Commander's gaze.

Wafer, who had been muttering in the ear of his neighbour, cleared his throat nervously. 'N-no, sir,' he stammered, too terrified to hold the man's gaze.

Nick glowered at him for several long moments, during which the others could almost feel the tension in the air around them, but after a while he looked away. 'Very well. I have no more time to waste on you.'

Oliver caught his breath, evidently relieved.

But Oliver's smile was quickly obliterated when, still glaring at no one in particular, Nick added, 'I merely thought that as all of the FF are on alert for any kind of suspicious behaviour, you might want to refrain from stepping out of line.' He smiled to himself as he said this, listening intently for his reaction.

No audible one came, however, so he continued to address the room at large, unaware of how white Wafer had turned at his words.

'Our objective is simple: to eliminate the bulk of The Inside government quickly and effectively, ahead of our assault on Samuel Brand himself. This is so that...'

He broke off as Wafer let out a petrified squeak, 'S-sir?'

Nick turned to face him once more. 'Yes?' he barked, irritated, 'what is it?'

'Sir, it is my... my belief that we are... we are being watched.' He jerked his head in the direction of the grimy window. 'L-look.'

As one, every FF agent swivelled round in their seats to gaze upon the middle-aged man lurking in the bushes behind them.

Nick was the first to his feet. 'Harper!' he bellowed, rounding on her. 'You told me you had surveillance around the place!'

'I did, sir!' she replied immediately, looking confused and panicked, 'I swear. Ten, maybe twenty men!'

The rest of the agents were standing up now, muttering warily to each other and surging towards the window.

'Stop!' Nick commanded, holding out his arms to prevent his colleagues advancing.

They obeyed at once, falling swiftly silent.

Nick pulled his hood up over his face, concealing it from view, before striding across the room, his hand snaking into his pocket and grasping the pistol inside. 'Stay where you are,' he breathed, glancing over his shoulder at the others, 'unless I order you otherwise; understand?'

They all nodded, and Nick leaned carefully against the window ledge, studying the watcher as he came closer, wide-eyed, pulling out his mobile as he did so. Nick felt his whole body tense up anxiously, but he relaxed as he watched the man's lips form a curse word and saw him stuff the phone back into his pocket. He had obviously failed to get a signal. With a start, he looked up and saw Nick watching him, gasped, turned on his heel and ran away at full pelt.

Nick whipped round with unnatural speed. 'Knight, Wafer, I want that man found. Bring him back here *alive*, got it? We need to find out what he knows.'

'Yes, Commander,' Luke and Oliver chorused. With that, they headed for the door.

Nick caught Oliver's eye. 'Don't let me down.'

EIGHTEEN

Layna listened to Delilah's footfalls grow fainter and fainter as the latter trudged along the corridor towards Nick's room, two floors below. Straining her ears, she heard the lift doors clang shut.

Quickly, she leapt off the end of her bed, dropping the forged papers she was supposed to be working on in her place, and then she pulled out her phone and dialled Zack's number.

He answered on the third ring. 'Hello?'

She smiled. 'Hi, you!'

'Hi' he echoed, the happiness in his voice evident. 'So, what's up? You OK?'

'Fine, thanks. You?'

He let out a long sigh. 'Stressed. I'm run off my feet; I don't think the office has ever received so many complaints!' He paused and took a deep breath. 'I'm so tired!' As if to prove the point, he yawned loudly.

Layna pulled a face. 'Poor you!' she sympathised.

He laughed wryly. 'Tell me about it!'

She opened her mouth to say something else, but then she heard footsteps coming back along the corridor towards her. 'Gotta go' she told Zack quickly, 'sorry.'

'OK, well, bye. Love you.'

'Love you too. See you later.'

She rang off hastily, just as Delilah entered the room, frowning.

'What're you doing?' Harper asked.

'Nothing,' Layna answered. 'Why?'

'No reason. I just wondered how you were getting on.' Delilah eyed the abandoned papers with raised eyebrows. 'Badly, obviously.' She sat on the end of the bed and picked them up. 'Fake ID documents?'

'Yeah.'

Delilah tutted. 'You'd better get them done before Nick gets here; he's on his way up now.'

'I thought he was calling Luke for a progress report on the search for that bloke who saw the meeting?'

'He's finished. Now he wants to refocus, talk about those Inside MPs he wants rid of and double our efforts to find the mole.'

'Right.' Layna's voice trembled slightly, but Delilah didn't notice.

'Here, get on with it,' the other woman advised, holding out the documents.

However, just as Layna was extending her hand to take them, Nick entered.

His eyes took in the scene before him and his face

darkened. 'I gave those to Layna to do, not you,' he told Delilah, an edge to his voice.

'I know, I was just about to—' Layna began.

'Wasn't talking to you, Layna,' Nick interrupted.

The colour rose in her cheeks and she nodded. 'Sorry.'

His expression did not soften. 'When I ask you to do a job, you do it; understand? It is essential that we keep ourselves well supplied with false IDs, in case we are discovered by The Inside government and need to justify ourselves. I will not tolerate a junior recruit like you compromising that task by disobeying my orders. Are we clear?'

'Yes, sir.'

'Good. Now take the documents down to my room and get on with your work. Off you go.'

Layna's eyes widened in surprise. 'Sir, I can finish them up here—'

'I've not come all the way up here to wait for you to finish a job that should have been completed hours ago!' he snapped, raising his voice. 'Off you go and don't get seen!' He gave her a push and she snatched her papers. 'Very well.' With that, she turned on her heel and left the room.

'That was a bit harsh,' Delilah told Nick after the door had closed. 'I mean, she was only taking a break.'

Nick nodded, stepping closer to her. 'I know. I wasn't really angry about that; I just wanted to talk to you alone.'

She looked surprised. 'Me? Why?'

Glancing at the door, he lowered his voice, as though he thought the room they were standing in was bugged. 'I think I can trust you.'

A flash of hurt crossed her face. 'What d'you mean "think"? Of course you can trust me!'

Unconcernedly, Nick shrugged. 'Whatever. I'm just saying that we can't trust everyone, especially not people like her.'

'You think Layna's the mole?'

For a long time, he didn't answer, his gaze travelling around the room. 'I don't know,' he admitted at last.

They fell silent, watching each other.

Delilah felt an odd pain in her chest as she looked at him, one that she couldn't quite define. Feeling suddenly awkward, she cleared her throat and brought the subject back round to the mole. 'So, what d'you suppose we do?'

'We have to crack down on security, make sure no one on The Inside has a hope of finding us and eliminate anyone who could be dangerous – anyone who's behaviour poses a threat to FF stability. Anyone who could be the mole.'

'Like Paul Broke? You got rid of him pretty quick.'

He nodded. 'Exactly. According to recent intelligence, he was working in league with our little traitor. So, it's lucky I acted when I did.' He didn't like lying to her, but he had heard the respect in her tone when she mentioned his actions with Broke and he detested the idea of losing that.

'So, who's next on your hit list?' Delilah asked after another pause. 'Layna?'

Nick shook his head, looking thoughtful. 'She's close to us. If it is her, all we've got to do is bide our time and watch. If she makes one move against us, we'll know.'

'OK, so if it isn't her, who else d'you reckon it could be?'

'Oliver Wafer for a start.'

'Really?' she asked, frowning slightly. 'Then why did you send him with Luke to go after that snoop?'

'Because if he turns out to be the mole, Luke can deal with the bastard before he can spill any valuable information on us to Insiders and ruin our organisation forever.'

'And if your instincts about him are wrong?'

'Then he'll have a chance to redeem himself; a chance he should be grateful for.'

Not quite sure what to say to this ominous statement, Delilah waited for him to say something else.

He took a long time to do so, but eventually told her, 'I don't know whether I'm right or not about Wafer. Just keep your eyes and ears open for anything or anyone suspicious.' He broke off, his dark eyes studying her face. It was impassive, as though she were trying to conceal from him what she was really thinking. Sighing, he turned away, not looking at her as he whispered, 'We are going to catch that mole, Delilah; mark my words.'

N

Layna's heart felt as though it was running a marathon. She had been eavesdropping on Nick and Delilah's conversation, and had heard every word they said. It was true that Nick wasn't sure if she was the mole or not, but he was getting suspicious and that was not the flawless image she'd been hoping for. Swallowing hard, she resolved to try much harder with her work in future. The ID documents slipped from her fingers, and she swore bitterly, stooping quickly to gather them up before the others heard the noise and came to investigate. With a sigh, she decided she had better put her new plan into action.

NINETEEN

Benjamin Rowler gave a deep sigh as, pulling the heavily graffitied maths book of one of his student's towards him, he prepared to start the agonisingly slow process of the night's marking. This was not an enviable task by anyone's standards, but it was especially laborious when you were as preoccupied as he was.

He hadn't been able to shake off the uneasy thoughts he'd had about the hooded man he had seen inside the old hotel. Could the man really be who he thought he was? If so, what had he been doing there? Why had he been watching him so intensely? What must be done about it?

He sighed again. It was no good, he would have to go to the police.

As he got to his feet, there was the sound of breaking glass from the conservatory. His heart pounding, he ran to investigate, a sickening sense of foreboding settling over him. His anxieties were well placed, for it was with a thrill of horror that he took in what he was seeing.

Shards of glass were strewn across the expensive mahogany flooring, as well as glass so fine that it looked like a sheet of white dust. The nearest window was little more than a bare frame. In the centre of the room lay a large brick. Upon its surface was written a single word: 'OUTSIDE'. Benjamin's frown deepened as he picked his way across the room and lifted the brick up; what did it mean? The word 'outside' could be telling him where the threat had come from or it could be an order from whomever had thrown it, telling him to leave the house. He glanced at the shattered window and thought, with a shudder, just how easily he could've been standing in its path. Swallowing hard, he tried to think. *What should I do?*

Without warning, a second brick shot through the opposite window, skimming the side of his head. Quickly, he dropped to his hands and knees, and immediately felt sharp pains as the glass sliced into his palms.

For what seemed to him like hours, he knelt there trembling while icy beads of sweat dripped from his forehead. Finally, putting up a hand to wipe them away, he gave a horrified start. Shockingly scarlet blood was running down from his temple.

When he had at last stopped shaking enough, he rose slowly to his feet with a half-formed plan to try to get some help swimming hazily in his mind. In the growing darkness, he fumbled for the conservatory door handle and staggered forwards, out into the cold night air.

'Help!' he shouted desperately as he made his way as quickly as he could up the deserted street. 'Help me, somebody, please!'

'Nobody can help you now,' hissed a soft, dangerously close voice. 'Nobody.'

Benjamin would have screamed, but a rough hand clamped over his mouth, stopping him from making a sound. A second hand, balled into a fist, made agonisingly painful contact with his head and, the next moment, there was darkness.

TWENTY

News of Mr Rowler's disappearance spread like wildfire through Inside High, and everyone had developed their own theories as to what had happened to him.

Some people guessed that he had run away from problems at home, while others suspected that he had suffered some sort of breakdown. The possibility of abduction occurred to barely anyone.

The truth was that those involved in the case of Benjamin Rowler were so secretive that only select members of the police force, the Brand family and Zack were supposed to know anything about it. Of course, this vow of silence was broken almost at once by Lucy and Zack, who couldn't resist divulging what they knew to the others, on the condition that they didn't mention it to a soul. Aside from this, however, the rules were stuck to.

This meant that, by the end of the week, Samuel's security office was so beset with letters from the general public demanding the facts of the incident that Zack found himself almost drowning in them. He was opening yet another batch – deciding which should be passed on to Samuel himself, and which simply filed away and forgotten about – when he spotted something on one of the letters that made his blood run cold. The black crest of the FF was emblazoned across the front of it and the address beside it made up of newspaper lettering. Biting down hard on his bottom lip, with his fingers trembling slightly, he broke the wax seal and started to read the letter, which was also composed of carefully assembled newspaper text:

> *Brand,*
>
> *This is your first and last chance. We want control of The Inside and all the perks included. If you don't step down, there will be trouble. Rowler is just the beginning. Next, we're coming for you. You have been warned.*

The note was unsigned.

Breathing fast, Zack reread it several times, certain phrases seeming to leap off the page. 'First and last chance', 'If you don't step down, there will be trouble' and 'You have been warned.'

Slowly, giving the impression of a calm he did not feel, he stood up – the note still clutched in his right hand. He knew he had to find Samuel as quickly as he could. This wasn't a minor irritation any more, it was serious. Deadly serious.

N

'I don't understand,' Nerrisia frowned as, a few hours later, she and the others sat on Lucy's bedroom floor, discussing the grim discovery. 'Why do they want control so much?'

'I bet it's my fault,' Bliss muttered darkly, glaring at the floor. 'I bet it's all for my mother's revenge.'

'Don't be stupid,' Sherona told her, shaking her head. 'They wouldn't do all this for revenge against you, not after all this time.'

Bliss scoffed at her. 'Yeah, they would. I'm Outside Enemy Number One.'

'But if it *is* just you they want, why are they coming after Dad?' Lucy asked. 'Why not kidnap *you* instead of Mr Rowler? Plus, there's Elodie and Bradley Close, where do *they* fit in to all this?'

'And what about the meeting Layna told us about? Where they talked about "eliminating the bulk of The Inside government". What's that got to do with you?' enquired Zack.

Bliss shrugged. 'I dunno.'

'I don't get any of this,' Liam grumbled, looking confused and agitated. 'It makes no sense!'

'Agreed,' Nerrisia sighed. 'There's no point dwelling on it though. Let's rehearse; we've got that gig at The Prince's Arms coming up and we've gotta be ready.'

Liam's face darkened still further. 'I'm not in the mood. The pay there is lousy anyway. Fifty quid for a three-hour set? It's inhumane!'

There was a bitter chorus of agreement at his words, from all except Lucy.

'You OK?' Nerrisia asked her.

With a start, Lucy looked round. 'What? Oh… yeah… yeah, I… I s'pose.'

They all looked thoroughly unconvinced and her pretence crumpled.

'No. I keep thinking about… about Dad,' Lucy wailed. 'I mean, look at the Close family. One mistake from Bradley, and he and Elodie end up dead, and their parents barely escape murder themselves. What… what if…' She broke off, shaking far too much to continue, her eyes wide and fearful.

'Oh, Lu,' Nerrisia sympathised, squeezing her hand tightly. 'It's OK.'

'Yeah,' Sherona added, 'nothing will happen. There's too much security around him for the FF to even get close.'

The others nodded, each giving her their own words of encouragement.

Then Liam stood up. 'Right' he declared firmly, 'I think some serious comfort food is in order. C'mon, let's go grab some pizza up town.'

'Is that all you think about, your stomach?' Lucy asked, traces of a smile flickering across her face.

'My stomach, my guitar and, first and foremost, my mates!' He grinned widely. 'Besides, eating gets us out of rehearsal for a couple hours. A definite plus point!'

'I'll second that,' Bliss agreed. 'Let's go!'

Together, they left the room. As they made their way downstairs, Lucy shot Liam a grateful look. He always managed to cheer her up – always. For some reason, her cheeks flushed slightly as she thought this and she quickly looked away.

Still, the feeling she'd encountered remained in the back of her mind and she couldn't stop herself wondering, even as they left the pizza restaurant hours later – was a friend all that Liam could be to her?

TWENTY-ONE

The room was dark and claustrophobic, smelling strongly of damp and rot. Nothing penetrated the area, aside from the feeble glare of a precariously hung, naked light bulb which swung dangerously to and fro. Benjamin was sitting with his back against the wall, his head lowered and his hands bound with rough lengths of rope. He was shaking uncontrollably.

Luke and Oliver bore down upon him, their sallow faces shielded from view by their hoods.

'Well?' Luke demanded venomously.

A series of incoherent mumblings were all that greeted his words.

This inflamed the rage already pounding through Knight's veins as he looked upon the cowering Insider. 'Speak up, you filthy Insider bastard! What did you *see*?'

'N-nothing,' Benjamin stammered, his feeble voice trembling as he looked up. 'I didn't see anything, I... I swear.'

Luke bent down and slapped him so hard that Rowler's head snapped back with huge force and he let out an agonised yelp.

'LIAR!' Knight bellowed. 'You're lying!'

'No!' Benjamin cried, 'I'm telling you the truth!'

'You know,' Oliver told him, his voice lower than Luke's, his tone oddly crossed between displeasure and understanding, 'we don't want to hurt you. Our aim is for equality, not domination. However...' He broke off and made a tutting noise through his teeth. 'If you won't tell us what you saw, then my colleague's little outburst was just the beginning, understand? So, do as we tell you and speak up!'

Swallowing hard, his heart pounding wildly in his chest, Benjamin tried again. 'I saw nothing!' he insisted, positively frantic now. 'Nothing!'

Luke took another step towards the prisoner, fiery danger etched into every line of his face. 'Feeling defiant, are we?' he asked, his rattling breath unbearably hot in Benjamin's ear. 'We'll soon fix that.' From inside his jacket pocket, he drew the silver knife that had been used to murder Elodie Close.

Eyes widening in sheer terror, Benjamin stared at Luke, cold sweat gushing from every pore of his body as he took in the dark-red stains covering the surface of the blade. He felt as though a bucket of ice cubes had been tipped down his back.

'Well?' Luke hissed, a smile slowly spreading across his face. 'Anything to say?'

✒

'Is that it?' Nick asked, pacing up and down the dingy hotel room, his every move studied intently by Oliver, Luke, Layna and Delilah. 'I mean, are you absolutely sure that's everything? *That's all that prat saw?*'

'Yes, sir,' Oliver replied.

'How can you be so sure?'

'He didn't exactly hold up well under torture. Had him sobbing in moments.' Oliver spoke with twisted humour. 'He even offered to give us Bliss Cookson's location, provided we let him go.'

'Did you?' The sudden urgency in his own voice surprised even Nick. '*Did you?*'

'What d'you take us for?' asked Luke tetchily. 'Bloody idiots? Course not; he'd be straight to the coppers. Insider scumbag! Info is good, but only if the source is. Besides, who's to say Rowler knew anything? He was probably spouting rubbish. We'll find the bitch in our own time. We've just gotta sort our immediate problems first, right?'

Nodding, Nick felt his breathing rate slowly return to normal. 'So, what did ya do?'

'Killed him,' answered Luke, his voice disgustingly casual. 'He'd given us what we needed.'

'And the body?' Nick continued sharply.

'Burned it' Luke replied, flicking the question away without pause.

Nick nodded again, but he said nothing more. For a reason he couldn't figure out, something Oliver had told him earlier was reverberating through his head: '*He even offered us Bliss Cookson's location'*. Had Rowler really known where to find Nick's sister? Had they really come that close to reaching her? The thought chilled him to the bone and that, above all else, disconcerted him.

It was Oliver who brought him back to the conversation. 'Rowler saw nothing too incriminating, nothing coppers could link to us anyway. So – even if he did blab about the meeting to someone and didn't tell us – we're not in too much danger. What do you suggest we do next, sir?'

'I… er… the mole. We'll move through darkness to cover our tracks, and then we crack down on security, got it? Once we've got the mole, we can go back to serious operations. We'll have to postpone our assault of Insider MPs 'til we're sure we're not being watched. Oliver, Luke – get the word out. Anyone who was at that meeting needs to know about plan B. Layna, get this place packed up and find us a new base; somewhere secluded and out of the way. Delilah, make a fresh set of fake ID in case things go totally pear-shaped.'

Delilah nodded. 'Right.'

'What about you, Nick?' Luke asked. 'Are you going to help?'

The accusatory edge to his voice made Nick slightly uncomfortable. 'Of course,' he replied coolly. 'I'll get some backup and set up some surveillance around our new location – once we've got one, of course.' His eyes flicked to Layna for a second; she held his gaze steadily. 'Does that satisfy you?' he asked the room at large.

Luke nodded curtly, but his expression seemed to darken still more. 'We'd better get a move on,' he told Oliver abruptly. 'Now.'

Wafer nodded, and they left without another word.

'What's his problem?' Delilah asked Nick, glaring at the door as it closed behind their two departed colleagues. 'Nobody speaks to you like that!'

'Yeah!' agreed Layna. 'He's got some nerve!'

Nick shrugged. 'Don't worry 'bout it' he told them. 'We've got more important things to think about.' He sighed bitterly as he spoke. Apparently, the stress the mole was causing at the FF was beginning to get to him.

Layna felt a fleeting stab of pity for him, but she pushed it away quickly and felt angry with herself. He had an extra member of his cell now, Wafer. If he was getting stressed, he could easily shift some of the workload onto him. Besides which, any disruption her presence in the FF could create ought to be cause for celebration. 'I should get started too,' she announced, more to distract herself from the moment of guilt than anything else. 'OK?'

'Sure,' Nick agreed, his tone becoming distracted again, 'I think I'll go down the pub; I need a drink.'

'You and me both,' said Delilah with an exasperated sigh. 'Mind if I join you before starting on those IDs?'

After considering her for a moment, Nick shook his head. 'You better not. If we're going to make a clean getaway, every second counts.'

She glared at him, eyes narrowing in defiance. 'Then why are you going for R and R while the rest of us get our arses in gear?'

Nick shrugged, wishing that she'd take the hint and leave him alone. 'I feel like it. Look, I'm in charge here, I thought you understood that!'

Deeply affronted, Delilah looked for a moment as though she was going to pursue the point, but, mercifully for him, she seemed to change her mind at the last moment. 'Fine!' she snapped, turning her back and striding away from him.

Nick gave a deep, bitter sigh, wincing slightly at the sound of the door slamming behind her.

Layna smiled ruefully as she turned to look at him. 'You OK?' she asked,

He nodded, irritation flashing across his face. 'I'm fine!' he snapped. 'Why wouldn't I be?' He glared at her, his eyes challenging. '*Well?*'

'I'm sorry,' she said slowly, 'I just thought—'

'Well, you thought wrong!' Anger was spitting out of him as though he were a poisonous snake, his voice rising with every acidic word. 'Haven't you got work to do?'

She nodded, lowering her gaze so that he couldn't see her raised eyebrows. 'I'll… I'll see you later then.'

'Yeah, whatever.' He cleared his throat gruffly, making his exit without another word.

Alone in the hotel room, Layna shook her head, mystified by all of them. How could she ever get used to this? Why was she even doing it? *For the greater good,* she told herself firmly. *For the good of The Inside.* She rolled her eyes at how melodramatic her thoughts sounded, before turning to the empty rucksack lying at the foot of her bed. Time to get started.

TWENTY-TWO

'Can I help you, mate?' The round-faced barman had a great, booming voice, the sound of which jerked Nick from his uneasy thoughts.

'What?' Nick muttered, looking up at him.

'Can I help you?' the man repeated. 'Or are you just gonna sit there all day?'

'Gin and tonic, sharpish.' Unsmiling, Nick returned his gaze to the counter; couldn't anyone see he wanted to be left alone?

The barman smiled, chuckling as he turned to pour the drink. 'Rough day?' he asked.

'Could say that.' Nick's words were forced through gritted teeth.

The barman didn't seem to notice Nick's tone, though, for he continued warbling as he slapped the glass in front of him. 'You and me both, mate. Just got off the phone with the bloody mother in law. She wants ferrying about once I've finished my shift. I ask you!' He took a swig from a dusty beer bottle and laughed bitterly before continuing.

'What does a bloke have to do to get a bit of sodding respect around here?'

Tuning out the inane carping, Nick allowed his mind to drift once more.

His father, Jordan Cookson, was a man for whom the whole of the FF had held a great deal of respect. Nobody had dared to question his judgement or orders, not even Nick. He had always prided himself on being utterly ruthless. In time, nobody dared oppose him. That was how the FF had accumulated so many followers during its first few years. Its leader had been both feared and idolised by Outsiders, and had seldom taken no for an answer.

While alive, Nick's father had impressed upon his young son every day that Insiders were not to be trusted and that their selfishness was what left families like the Cookson's to scrape by on almost nothing. That was why they had to fight back, he'd explained, to end the segregation. Weakness, Jordan had said, was not an option. Any weak links in the chain of FF activists had to be eliminated quickly before the whole chain fell apart.

Growing up with his father's radical behaviour and beliefs meant that Nick, too, was not a man who often put up with an attitude such as the one Luke had shown earlier, as his treatment of Paul Broke had demonstrated. Ordinarily, Luke would have met with the same fate. So why had Nick, against everything his father had taught him, allowed Luke to get off so lightly with his insubordination?

The frown on Nick's face deepened as the question he had fought to suppress since he had entered the pub finally came to the forefront of his mind. Though he would never admit it, the truthful answer was that he didn't want to cross Lucas Knight.

Luke had passed the exceptionally complex FF training programme with flying colours in less than two months before climbing to the position of third in command in record time, constantly evading police capture along the way. You didn't get that far that quickly without discarding any desire for sentimentality, and Nick was willing to bet that their history together would count for nothing if he got on Luke's bad side. *Besides,* he told himself, *it's never happened before, what's the likelihood of it happening again?*

He drained his glass and slammed it back onto the bar.

The noise stopped the still-ranting barman in his tracks. 'Refill?' he asked, with a start of surprise.

'Nah.' Nick dug around in his wallet and placed a five-pound note on the counter. 'Does that about cover it?'

Without waiting for a response, Nick got to his feet and headed for the door.

TWENTY-THREE

'I have to admit that was a wicked audience!' Bliss announced, as she and the others collected their belongings from the makeshift green room at the back of The Prince's Arms after their set.

Sherona was retying her hair in a fresh ponytail. 'Yeah,' she agreed, 'I really got the feeling they were enjoying themselves – like they wanted us to keep playing.'

'I love it when that happens,' Nerrisia mused, her face lighting up at the thought. 'It makes all the practise worthwhile.'

Leaning heavily against the far wall, Zack stifled a yawn behind his hand. 'For you maybe. I'm knackered!' He laughed, but it sounded oddly hollow, and his friends looked at him with concern. His face was unusually pale, throwing the dark shadows under his eyes into horribly vivid relief. He was also looking thinner than they'd ever seen him, as if the smallest force would send him crumpling to the floor.

'You OK, mate?' enquired Liam, frowning.

'I'm fine.' Zack's smile looked more like a grimace, but he stood up straighter. 'I just... need to crash.'

Liam nodded. 'You and me both! Are you guys still OK to come to mine tonight?'

A murmur of assent came back to him.

He grabbed his bag and headed for the exit. 'C'mon, no time like the present.'

Just as they were closing the door behind them, Liam's mobile rang. As he checked the caller details, the habitual good humour of his expression evaporated. 'You have *got* to be kidding me!' he groaned.

'What's up?' asked Bliss curiously. 'Is it your mum?'

'No' Liam snarled, his teeth suddenly gritted, 'Rebecca.'

'Rebecca!' her incredulous exclamation was followed by a snort of laughter. '*Rebecca*?'

'Shut up!' Liam hissed, and to his friends' bewilderment, he put the phone to his ear. 'Becks, hi...'

'Becks?' Bliss mouthed, her eyebrows skyrocketing as she looked at the others, each of whom was mirroring her expression. Lucy cleared her throat loudly.

Glancing around at them, Liam flushed. 'Um... look, I'd better get going... No, it's not that I don't like talking, I just... yeah, I know, but... yeah... OK, um... bye...' He hung up quickly and turned to face the others. 'Not a word!' he spat at them.

'Since when has Rebecca Bamforth been "Becks"?' asked Nerrisia. 'And since when has she had your number?'

'Since the maths homework thing,' Liam mumbled. At the looks on their faces, he rushed on. 'She wanted it in case she needed to check anything!'

'Check anything? Is that what they're calling it now?' Zack asked, laughing at his friend's humiliated expression, his weariness quite forgotten.

Liam gave him a shove. 'Shut it!' he snapped.

Nerrisia shook her head at both of them and turned instead to Bliss. 'What about the Sunnyside curfew?' she asked, frowning slightly. 'Are you sure you should be coming with us? Isn't it against the rules or—'

'Oh, *come on*, Nerris!' Bliss interrupted, with a half-frustrated, half-beseeching look in her direction. 'Give me a break! You sound like the head care worker! You're my friends; I'm coming with you, OK?'

Nerrisia's frown deepened and she opened her mouth as though she wanted to protest further, but she was prevented from doing so by Sherona. 'Are we going or not?' the latter cut in quickly.

Liam nodded, glad of her quick thinking. 'Let's go.'

*

As they headed through the bar and out onto the street, with Nerrisia and Bliss still bickering about Bliss's breach of curfew – Lucy hung back with an uncharacteristically sour expression on her face. *Liam has Rebecca Bamforth's phone number.* The thought made her stomach muscles clench uncomfortably. She couldn't believe he had taken this long to tell her about it. Without her knowledge, her hands balled into fists. He was supposed to be her best friend – what was he playing at?

She stopped herself right there, blushing to the roots of her hair. What did it matter that he hadn't mentioned it? *He* didn't blow a gasket every time *she* gave someone her phone number, so why on earth should she care about what he did with his?

Because Rebecca Bamforth isn't just someone.

The thought was there before she could stop it, and – despite knowing that none of the others could hear her internal monologue – the colour in her face redoubled. A horrible image was now swimming hazily to the forefront of her mind: Liam and Rebecca, beaming at each other and walking up the street holding hands. Lucy shuddered and pushed it firmly away. She was being an idiot – that would never happen. Would it?

✦

'Liam, mate, just switch the bloody thing off!' pleaded Zack, glaring at Liam's mobile, which hadn't stopped ringing since the friends had left the gig an hour and a half ago. 'It's doing my head in!'

'Sorry!' Liam sighed irritably and seized his phone. 'I wish she'd leave me alone, really I do, but she's after me and won't let up! She just doesn't want to hear that I'm not interested.'

'So?' Bliss looked distinctly nonplussed. 'Just tell her straight: "You're a freak, keep out of my life." It's not hard!'

'As always, your compassion and sensitivity shine through!' said Sherona with a sardonic smile.

In response, Bliss rolled her eyes so dramatically that everyone fell about laughing.

They only stopped when Jason, Skye's twin brother, poked his head round Liam's bedroom door and told them to, 'shut up or else!'

'Loser,' Liam muttered darkly as the door slammed behind his brother, 'Skye doesn't care if we have a good time. Jase doesn't either; he's only doing it to wind me up.'

Nerrisia looked hopelessly at the closed door. 'Great,' she sighed, thinking of the baby that was currently screaming his head off at home, 'in eleven years' time, this'll be happening to me too!'

Liam shook his head. 'You'll have trouble long before then; he's been giving me grief since he could crawl. Brace yourself, Nerris; life as you know it will be over before long.'

Nerris buried her face in her hands with a moan of despair. Lucy threw Liam a withering look as she put an arm around her shoulders.

'Just saying,' he muttered, looking bemused. 'She's gotta be prepared.'

'Besides,' Zack interjected, seeing the potential for another argument to develop and feeling far too tired to submit to it, 'you won't need to put up with it for that long. Before you know it, you'll be at uni and then you're home free.' For a second, an expression of deepest wistfulness crossed his face, but it was gone just as swiftly as it had appeared. *Don't,* he told himself firmly. *Don't even go there, Zackary.*

Nerrisia looked slightly happier, but was clearly still fed up. She looked around the room at the others. 'Is anyone else tired? Think I'm gonna turn in.'

'Me too,' Sherona agreed, stretching.

The others nodded in agreement and soon Liam was lying in bed, with the others spread out on the floor around him.

His eyes rested on his phone, which was lying discarded a few inches away. Who knew how many missed calls he would have from Rebecca when he switched it on in the morning? Rolling over and closing his eyes, he decided the only comfortable thing to do was ignore it. After all, she couldn't possibly keep it up for much longer – nobody could be that dense. In a few minutes, the newly optimistic Liam was fast asleep.

Rebecca's pursuit of Liam was not far from Lucy's mind either, but she could not let it go so easily. She couldn't stop thinking about how persistent Bamforth was being in her relentless quest for Liam's affection. It was so possessive. She shuddered and felt a prickle of red-hot anger run across her skin. If Rebecca kept pushing for what she wanted, Liam was sure to begin feeling bad about ignoring her and give in. After that, Rebecca would have him right where she wanted him.

Once again, the image of Liam and Rebecca hand in hand flashed across Lucy's mind's eye. Face burning, she blinked furiously in an attempt to clear it and tried to force herself to focus on something else. *Stop being paranoid,* she told herself angrily. *You're being really overprotective. If Liam wants to date anyone, he has the sense to avoid freaks like Bamforth.*

Feeling slightly better, she turned over and closed her eyes. *Besides,* she thought muzzily, as she at last felt herself falling asleep, *who in their right mind would fancy Liam Smith?*

TWENTY-FOUR

Sherona sat at the desk in her bedroom, trying and failing to focus on her history essay. It was no good, however; she was far too preoccupied to concentrate.

Stretching, she turned her attention to what was really on her mind. Just over a week had elapsed since the performance at The Prince's Arms, and life had become increasingly stressful ever since.

Samuel was continuing to receive anonymous threatening messages, each more aggressive than the last. As a result, he, Lucy and Rosa had all become increasingly withdrawn and anxious.

Zack, too, was feeling the strain of the constant stream of hate mail, as he was the one left to handle it all. Though he would never admit it to the others, it was clear to all of them that he was also pining for Layna, whom he had not seen in weeks and was missing terribly.

Sherona's thoughts travelled to Liam, who – despite not receiving threatening messages in the way Samuel was – had resorted to keeping his phone permanently switched off in order to stop Rebecca Bamforth calling and texting him. Not being forward enough to confront her about it, he had nowhere to hide at school, where Rebecca would trail around after him and the others as soon as they were released from lessons, constantly making excuses to join in with their conversations, while batting her eyelashes and shooting Liam wide, over-enthusiastic grins at every opportunity. Her behaviour was making everyone irate – Lucy in particular.

She was short-tempered and crabby whenever she spoke with Liam in Rebecca's presence and often elected to ignore him completely when they were with the others. He remained ignorant of the reasons behind her behaviour, and this was making the whole situation much worse, as his bewilderment made him depressed and sulky.

Their friends' constant misery made it very difficult for the others to make interesting conversation. It was getting so tiresome that – most days – Bliss, Nerrisia and Sherona resorted to cutting Lucy and Liam out of their discussions completely. When they all trooped despondently into Lucy's house every evening after school, Zack was not much help to ease the discomfiture.

Now, Sherona pushed back her essay in defeat; she had no chance of finishing her homework tonight. Getting to her feet, she walked over to her stereo and pressed play.

Quietly, she began to sing under her breath, seizing her hairbrush from the bedside table and using it as a microphone. Closing her eyes, she imagined she was performing, not at a small, semi-dodgy pub crammed with tipsy punters but in a packed-out stadium filled with screaming fans. She smiled to herself at the thought, and her voice rose as she gained in confidence.

'Bravo!'

Her eyes flew open and her face flushed with embarrassment. 'Dad!' she cried in horror, seeing her father standing just behind her. 'What're you playing at?'

Alan Hamilton chuckled at his daughter's indignation, but he did his best to look wide-eyed and innocent. 'I'm not playing at anything!' he protested, 'I'm just listening to my superstar singer partying it up, making her old man the proudest dad in the world. That's not a crime is it?'

She gave him a shove. '*Dad!*'

'What is it, my little superstar? Name your desire, and I shall make it come about!'

'Stop mucking around!' she told him, rolling her eyes, 'I was trying to concentrate!' She switched off the CD player and glared at her father, her arms folded. 'Haven't you got anything better to do?'

He sighed heavily. 'Alas, I do!' he announced, grinning. Seeing the look on Sherona's face, he dropped the act at last. 'OK, OK. See you downstairs for dinner in ten minutes, all right?' He headed for the door but hesitated just before he reached it, turning back to face her. 'I really am proud of you, you know,' he said seriously. 'You have a beautiful voice – just like your mum.'

A wistful expression came over his face, and he glanced at the gold-framed photograph on Sherona's desk. Alice, his beloved wife, had shared her daughter's auburn ringlets, and they had had the same piercing stare. The same way of making him feel that they could see right into his head. Right into his soul.

The night his wife had been taken from him had been the worst night of Alan's life.

Alice, a senior carer at The Inside Hospice, had been driving home from her weekly night shift when her car had skidded on black ice and collided with an oncoming Range Rover. She had been killed instantly.

'Dad?'

He blinked in surprise as he felt Sherona's hand on his forearm. 'Yes, love?'

'You OK?' His daughter's eyes had rounded with concern.

'What, me? Of course,' he forced a smile. 'I was just thinking.' Shaking himself, he gave her a squeeze. 'You're a good kid; you know that?'

She grinned. 'Cheers.'

They stood in silence for a long while, each of them lost in their own thoughts, before at last Sherona spoke.

'Love you, Dad,' she whispered.

'I love you too, kiddo,' he replied, kissing her lightly on the top of the head. 'You've no idea how much.' With a heavy sigh, Alan left the room.

Sherona looked from the empty space where her dad had stood moments before to the photograph of her mum standing in pride of place on her desk. Her parents loved her so much, and she loved them ten times more in return. Nothing – be it her dad's infuriating antics or her mum's untimely death – would ever change that.

A picture of Bliss flashed suddenly into her mind, and she felt an unexpected rush of pity for her best friend. She couldn't imagine what it must be like to have one parent dead and the other at the top of The Inside's most-wanted list. It must be so difficult. *How,* she wondered, *can any parent despise their own child enough to be plotting their murder? Why would any parent even consider committing such a despicable act?* She shook her head – there was no point trying to understand Outsiders. Nobody knew how their minds worked. Nobody ever would.

TWENTY-FIVE

'Please, sir, penny for a poor child?'

Nick looked down to see where the tremulous voice was coming from and recoiled at the speed of light.

Sitting on the ground before him was a small, ashen-faced child, whose pallid skin did nothing to hide her protruding ribs. Her skeletal frame was clothed only in thin, grey rags, stained with grease, mud and – it was with a thrill of horror that Nick saw it – liberal amounts of dried blood. Her grey eyes were deadened and soulless; all hope had left them. The girl's only other possession was a limp, wretched-looking teddy bear – whose threadbare fur was also covered in filth – clutched tightly in her tiny hand.

The girl was hunched up against the bitter wind and her blue lips trembled as she spoke. 'Please, sir, penny for a poor child?'

Gathering himself, Nick bent down so that he was level with her. 'What's happened to you? Where are your parents?'

'I ain't got no parents, sir,' she replied, her wispy voice barely enough to combat the gale whipping up all around them. 'Me ma died not long after I were born, so they say. She weren't strong enough to cope with life on The Outside. She didn't always live 'ere, ya know, but she did bad stuff to get money for us and me pa turned 'er in to the Insiders.'

Nick clenched his fists, shaking with fury. This story was one he had heard countless times as he travelled the streets of The Outside, but it never failed to provoke a reaction in him. Every time he thought of Samuel Brand, with his fancy house and his happy family, it made him feel physically sick with rage.

The girl on the floor coughed loudly, regaining Nick's full attention.

He pulled his wallet out of his trouser pocket and passed it to her. 'Here,' he told her quickly, 'keep it.'

She gasped, staring at it as though it were the Holy Grail. 'Thank you, sir.' Her efforts to raise her voice made her cough again and she broke off, shivering violently.

Hastily, Nick took off his jacket, draping it around her shoulders. 'You wanna watch that cough,' he said as he did so, 'and get some medicine or something.'

'I ain't got time nor money for medicine, sir,' the girl replied, her voice resigned, 'and it wouldn't do no good now anyways, I'm dyin'.' She tried to pull Nick's coat tighter around herself, but her arms were too thin and weak. Giving up, she put her head on her knees and groaned softly.

As he watched her, Nick felt as though a fragment of steel had entered his soul. *How could anyone let this happen? How could anyone allow such suffering?* He cleared his throat. 'Don't worry,' he mumbled, 'you're going to be OK.' Both of them knew that they were empty words, but he had nothing else to offer her.

With what was clearly an Olympian effort, the girl raised her head slightly, a ghost of a smile flickering across her face. 'You a Freedom Fighter, sir?' she asked, her voice becoming even more feeble. 'You wanna stop the Insiders havin' everythin'?'

Nick laughed. 'Yeah, I am a Freedom Fighter. How did ya know?'

'Most folk jus' walk on by when I ask 'em for stuff; they think I'm beyond help. But not the Freedom Fighters,' she wheezed, breaking off into a gargantuan coughing fit before she was able to continue.

The sickening sound filled Nick's ears and made him wince involuntarily.

'Freedom Fighters ain't the type to give up, sir; they keep fightin'. You gonna keep fightin', sir?' the girl enquired softly, when at last she was able to speak once more.

'Yeah.' This time, he spoke with absolute conviction, his voice rising with heartfelt passion. 'You can be sure of that, I promise.'

She nodded. 'Thank you, sir,' she repeated, eyelids flickering like lame butterflies, 'and good luck to ya.'

They looked at each other for a long moment, and then Nick gave a deep sigh and started to walk away. However, he had only taken a few steps when the girl's shaking voice called him back.

'Is it nice, where I'm goin'?' she asked, glancing up at the overcast sky above them. 'Is it all right there, do ya s'pose, sir?'

He felt his throat constrict and his heart sink horribly. 'Yeah,' he croaked, swallowing hard, 'I… I think so.'

Her expression was no longer pained and sickly. Instead, she looked serenely up at him, her eyes slightly brighter. 'Better than here,' she murmured. 'Better than this.' With that, she closed her eyes, and began rocking slowly backwards and forwards, humming softly to herself.

Unable to look at the little girl any more, Nick began to power walk up the street towards the dilapidated building that was now his cell's headquarters. He bowed his head low.

The girl could not have been more than eight years old, and her life was already fading away. She was so badly malnourished that it was nothing short of a miracle she had survived this long, being forced to live the way she had. She had only days left at most, but it was clear to Nick that she was highly unlikely to survive the night, which was forecast to be cruelly cold.

Swift, burning anger pulsed through his veins at the thought of the girl, so hopelessly alone in this dark, demeaning world. Anger at Samuel Brand, for allowing all this extensive injustice to take place in a country he was supposed to be running, while he lived the high life with his shallow, woefully ignorant wife and spoiled brat of a daughter. Anger at Bradley Close and all the other worthless traitors who had attempted to thwart the FF's fight for justice. But the one who infuriated and embittered him beyond all others – so much that he could barely contain himself – was the FF mole. The person who was happily spilling FF secrets to The Inside government and laughing at his or her handiwork as the whole of the organisation was thrown into complete turmoil.

Lengthening his stride, he increased his speed while listening to the blood roaring in his ears. He wanted to get back to Luke, Layna, Oliver and Delilah, and formulate some form of new strategy to discover the mole's identity. The list of suspects was extensive and extremely difficult to narrow down. Still, Nick's hunger for action had increased tenfold since his meeting with the beggar girl, and he needed to feel he was doing something – *anything* – to help others like her; no matter how long it took.

TWENTY-SIX

'I dunno 'bout this, Luke,' Oliver admitted, his voice uncertain. 'It's not what the FF is supposed to be about.'

With his back turned away from his pitiful excuse for an ally, Luke rolled his eyes, irritated by how slow Oliver was being.

He didn't respond to Wafer's comment immediately, electing instead to pace the bedroom for several minutes before he even made eye contact, his footsteps echoing off the crumbling walls around them. 'Yeah, right,' he scoffed at last, with a loud, mocking laugh.

'Huh?' Oliver asked, frowning in confusion. An edge of tetchiness crept into his voice as he continued. 'Why the sarcasm? You know I'm right. The FF stands up for what's right, for equality between Insiders and Outsiders – to get everyone on level pegging – not to slaughter every Insider in sight!'

Luke laughed again, stopping by the window and slowly running his fingers along the cracked, grimy sill. 'Says who?' he asked softly.

Oliver opened and closed his mouth for several minutes, struggling to find an answer. Eventually, however, he shrugged his shoulders. 'That's what I joined for.'

Rolling his eyes again, Luke turned to look at him, his expression derisive. 'I've got news for you,' he sneered. 'You're living in a dreamworld. Insiders will never give us level pegging by choice – they're too damn arrogant – if we want it, we've gotta take it by force.'

'If you say so,' Oliver conceded, 'but I still reckon you should've asked Nick before you sent those letters to Brand. He's gonna hit the roof when he finds out.'

'Who says he ever *will* find out?' Luke replied, a cruel smile twisting his thin lips. 'Who says he's even going to be around here much longer?'

There was something in Luke's voice that made a prickle of foreboding run across Oliver's skin. 'What're you on about?' the latter asked, glancing around apprehensively, as though he expected the room to be bugged. 'If someone hears you...' he broke off, knowing his words were falling on deaf ears; settling instead for an exasperated sigh.

Luke, his smile still in place and his eyes lighting up with malice, took one step closer and spoke in confidential tones. 'I'm talking about the fact that he's a totally incompetent leader, he's never pulled the trigger in his life and he only passed the training programme because it was his father's dying wish for him to take over at the FF. His mother would make a much better leader than him.' He paused for breath, his wicked grin widening. 'Or, at least, that's what I'll tell her when I bust her out of jail, also dropping in the tiny detail that I have succeeded in forcing Samuel Brand out of control. She'll then make me her right-hand man and I'll get my chance to climb the FF's ladder and then…' He let out a cackle of insane laughter, leering at Oliver and clapping his hands together at the thought of what was to come. 'And then, when the time is right, I'll take my place at the head of the Freedom Fighters organisation, you just see if I don't.'

Oliver stared at him in surprise and then blinked at him in bemusement for a long while before raising a quizzical eyebrow. 'And you want my help?' he asked at last.

'I can't break Salina Cookson out of prison by myself, can I? Delilah and Nick were mates when they were kids, so she won't be any help against him, then there's Layna, but she's such a coward that she wouldn't dare contradict his orders. I need reinforcements.'

Seeing the unconvinced look on Oliver's face, he quickly continued. 'Imagine it, mate, us in charge of the whole of the FF, us living the high life for a change!' He paused dramatically, studying Wafer intently with his ice-blue gaze, a challenging glint in his eye. 'You up for it?'

'I dunno…' Oliver replied uncertainly, though his tone contained traces of temptation, 'it seems a bit risky—'

'Oh, come on!' Luke urged, frustration making his voice rise to a high volume. 'Think of the glory! We'd be responsible for a revolution! All the FF has worked for, all down to us!'

He was a very passionate and persuasive speaker, and Oliver couldn't resist the inducement anymore.

'OK' he agreed, 'I'll do it.'

A sly smile spread across Luke's pale face; it was all coming together. Predictably, Wafer had fallen for his talk of shared glory and, whenever he wavered, it would be a useful carrot to dangle in front of him to ensure he followed orders. Of course, an alliance was not something Lucas Knight set much store by, and, when Oliver had served his purpose, this particular agreement would have to be terminated. *No matter,* he thought to himself. *By that time, I – Lucas Knight – will be untouchable.*

N

Outside the door, pressed firmly against the wall that separated him from Luke and Oliver, Nick felt as though a bucket of ice cubes had been tipped down his back. It couldn't be true; it couldn't possibly be true. His heart was hammering painfully against his ribcage; his breath shallow and panicky. Suddenly, he became aware that he was shaking.

Go in there now, he told himself, trying to force movement into his trembling legs. *Go in there and kill them both.* But, as his hand moved down to retrieve a gun from his pocket, he realised that his jacket, along with his weapon, was still wrapped around the shoulders of the little girl. He was defenceless; if he attempted to retrieve a gun from anywhere inside the building, Wafer and Knight were sure to realise what was going on and kill him before he could do anything. He had no choice but to pretend he had heard nothing of their conversation and pray he was mistaken. *Please,* he thought desperately, feeling a layer of sweat break out all across his body, *please let me be wrong.*

TWENTY-SEVEN

'Where do you think you're going?' Nick asked suspiciously, his eyes narrowing as he regarded Layna, whose hand had just grasped the door handle. 'You can't just walk out of here, ya know.'

Layna raised her eyebrows at his prickly tone. 'Can't I? I've got nothing to do round here, and Delilah's got the afternoon off; I might as well leave too.'

A splutter of wry laughter escaped Nick's lips. 'You've got an attitude, Johns,' he told her dryly, 'I'm in charge here!'

She nodded. 'True, but I have worked my arse off over the past few weeks, surely I'm entitled to a bit of respite?' She smiled innocently, hoping her daring would pay off. She hadn't been able to get away from the FF for what seemed like forever, and she thought that if she didn't get to see Zack soon, she might go mad from loneliness. Just the idea of him made her smile, but they hadn't spoken in weeks and she was really missing him. Of course, she couldn't tell Nick this, so all she could do was wait for his answer. 'Well?' she asked, a hint of audacity in her voice.

Sighing deeply, Nick glanced apprehensively over his shoulder. Luke was in the next room, no doubt whispering with Oliver about how to bring about his downfall and he didn't much fancy being left alone with them, despite the fact he had now replenished his supply of easily reachable weapons and could pull one out in the blink of an eye. He shook his head. 'Stay. I could use your help on something.'

'What?'

'I… er…' He cast around to try to find something to say, but no stroke of inspiration came to him. 'I…' he trailed off, the colour fast rising in his cheeks.

Layna surveyed him; scepticism etched into her features. 'You haven't got a reason for keeping me back, have you?' she asked, raising her eyebrows.

Defeated, he shrugged his shoulders. 'Forget it,' he muttered. 'Take the rest of the day off.'

'Thank you!' she smiled in relief and, without another word, left him alone in the room.

As he watched the door close behind her, Nick felt all his senses sharpen considerably. He was never one to let down his guard, but now, alone with two known killers for whom he feared he was the next target, he could not relax for a nanosecond. That would surely be suicidal. Practical thinking was what was needed here; there was no point panicking prematurely. If he allowed himself to become paranoid too quickly, he would be all the more vulnerable to attack, and vulnerability was something his father had taught him never to demonstrate.

He started to pace the room, listening to his own footfalls – using the slow, steady rhythm to calm his nerves and clear his mind. *What to do?*

First and foremost, he must make absolutely sure that what he had heard several days ago, when he had returned to headquarters after his meeting with the girl, had been correct. After all, it was wrong and insurmountably foolish to accuse members of his own cell of treachery without concrete proof, and he had been somewhat distracted that night to say the least. Though he was loath to admit it, the story of the girl's plight had got to him, and his judgement had no doubt been clouded by emotion. He must be sure before he took action.

Stopping abruptly, he found himself facing the door behind which Luke and Oliver still lurked. Despite his own assurances that they were likely to pose no threat, he felt a jolt of fresh uncertainty at the sight of it and found himself wondering if he was kidding himself.

There was no denying that Luke's attitude towards him had changed over recent months. He was often heard remarking on FF protocol, his manner sometimes flippant and usually snide. This unsettled Nick more than he had let on. Perhaps being third in command was no longer enough for Luke. Nick was chilled by this thought, and so he turned his attention to assessing his second potential adversary.

Unlike Knight, Oliver Wafer had barely scraped through the FF training programme. His intelligence was of no great quantity and his fieldwork was mediocre at best – but that was no reason to discount him from being a possible threat. The man had been embarrassed in front of many influential members of the Freedom Fighters community, courtesy of Nick's actions at the meeting watched by Benjamin Rowler, and this – he thought – could be a reason for Wafer to harbour a vendetta against him. People had been butchered for far less on The Outside, after all.

Alone, Oliver Wafer was a blithering fool who could do no more to influence the FF than the beggar girl Nick had encountered on the street, but with Luke by his side he had a much higher chance of success. Oliver may be a weakling, but he was at least determined, and if he was offered the right reward, he was more than happy to take risks. No, Oliver could not be ignored.

Without warning, the door in front of him was thrown open, and Luke was standing just a few yards away, with Oliver directly behind him.

'Hello,' Luke purred, his tone cold as an icecap. 'Didn't know you were here.'

'I don't have to let you know my every move, Lucas,' Nick replied, trying to sound just as coolly indifferent as Knight had.

'Lucas?' he sneered, taking a threatening step towards him. 'Since when have I been Lucas?'

'What does it matter? My point is, I don't trust you with every little detail of how I spend my time, and it is not your place to question me.'

'Temper, temper,' Luke mocked. 'No need to be so fierce. I wasn't questioning you, merely expressing my... surprise.' He lingered menacingly on the last word, and it hung in the air around them, which had suddenly become full of tension. 'I don't like surprises,' he murmured.

'What?' Nick held his gaze steadily, but Luke's words had quickened his pulse, and he felt his hands slowly clenching up in his pockets. 'What are you talking about?'

'They're funny things, you see. You never know when they're going to sneak up on you. Grab hold of you. Shock you.'

Luke was so close now that Nick could see silvery flecks of spit flying from his chapped lips. Involuntarily, Nick took a step back.

Luke smirked still more. 'Catch my drift?' he asked softly.

Gritting his teeth and squaring his shoulders, Nick raised his chin, and puffed his chest out; his lip curling into a snarl. '*Was that a threat?*'

'No, no,' Luke answered coolly, 'just some friendly advice'.

Motioning for Oliver to follow him, Luke strode confidently across the room, stopping just as he reached the door and turning back to glare at Nick one more time. 'Here's a second piece of friendly advice: not a word of this to anyone. Got it?' Soundlessly, he opened the door and was gone.

It felt as if Nick's mind and body had gone into meltdown. He stood rooted to the spot, his chest rising and falling in rapid, anguished pants as he tried to make sense of what had just happened. Swallowing hard, he forced himself to focus on the facts of the situation.

One thing was certain, Luke's departing words had – whatever he might say – been a threat. Luke was not the type to threaten people lightly. This whole thing had suddenly got serious. The stakes had been raised, and Nick knew that – from now on – there was no way he was admitting his terror to anyone. From now on, he was on his own.

TWENTY-EIGHT

The pounding in Zack's head was almost unbearable.

The phone had been ringing non-stop for the past three days, and he was absolutely exhausted. It didn't help that every single phone call was made by rude, arrogant and ill-informed members of the public, all of whom insisted on grilling him for non-existent information on the still-missing Benjamin Rowler. If he had to explain to one more pretentious member of the populace that the investigation into Rowler's disappearance was strictly confidential, and that any citizen who had a direct link to Rowler or could supply any new information on the case should contact the police directly, he would explode.

Closing his eyes tightly, he began counting from one to ten in his head, taking deep, calming breaths as he did so and saying a silent prayer that when he opened them the room would have stopped spinning. *No point getting stressed about it,* he told himself as he prepared to face the phone again. *People have got a right to know and you'll just have to put up with it. It's not as though it's a great hardship or anything; just answer the phone, and deal with each call calmly and professionally. No big deal.*

Just as he was opening his eyes, the doorbell rang.

'Zack!' Samuel bellowed from the floor above. 'Can you get that, please? I'm expecting Mrs Pollington to call in!'

Positive thinking flew out the window, and Zack put his head in his hands. 'Not her,' he groaned. '*Please*, not her.'

Relentlessly, the bell continued to ring, and Zack had no choice but to grit his teeth, force a smile onto his face and drag his reluctant feet into the hallway. Bracing himself, he heaved the door open. 'Hello?' he mumbled wearily, without looking up, 'May I help you?'

'Hey, stranger.'

His face brightened at once at the sound of Layna's voice. 'Hi,' he beamed with sudden enthusiasm. 'God, am I glad to see you!'

She must have heard the note of relief in his tone because a concerned frown flitted onto her face. 'Who're you expecting?'

'Nobody, don't worry about it.'

'No, tell me,' she insisted. 'Something's up; you look shattered!'

Sighing deeply, he saw that there was no point trying to keep up the pretence. 'I am,' he admitted. 'Work's really full on at the moment.' Shrugging, he tried his hardest not to sound self-pitying as he added, 'I guess I should be used to it by now.'

Layna felt a pang of sympathy for him but she was now curious too. 'Why?' she asked as he stepped over the threshold towards her. 'What's been going on?'

'There's been a disappearance,' Zack replied, a shadow instantly falling across his face. 'The bloke who's gone missing is Benjamin Rowler. He was a teacher up at the school – you know, Inside High – so pretty much everyone knows about it. The letters and phone calls are flooding in.'

It was as though someone had taken Layna's guts in their ice-cold hands and twisted them into the most agonising knot imaginable. Black spots began appearing at the edges of her vision, and she felt her breathing become ragged and shallow. Her throat tightened to an unbearable degree, and when she next spoke her voice was hoarse and shaky. 'Oh… Oh God…'

At once, Zack's expression became even more anxious. 'Baby, are you all right?'

His words seemed to be coming from far, far away, and Layna had to fight against the waves of blinding dizziness that were now crashing continuously over her in order to give him a reply that was virtually incoherent. 'Rowler… dead…. tortured… murdered. Oh my God!' Before she could say another word, she dissolved into desperate, despairing sobs, tears cascading down her cheeks like a waterfall.

Without warning, her legs gave way, and Zack only just managed to stop her falling to the hard, cold concrete of the ground below. She continued to moan and weep, unintelligible words tumbling one after the other from her mouth.

All Zack could do was whisper soft, consoling words. 'It's all right,' he soothed. 'It's OK; I've got you.'

As much as she longed to believe his words, Layna simply could not bring herself to do so. What the FF had done to Benjamin Rowler had haunted her nightmares ever since Luke and Oliver had recounted the events to herself, Nick and Delilah over a month ago, and – as yet – she had been unable to relive them for anyone. But if there was anybody in the world she would choose to share the subject of her night terrors with, it was Zack. *Besides*, she reminded herself, *at some point it has to be done*. She took a deep breath, swallowed repeatedly in an attempt to rid herself of the rock-hard lump of tears still lodged firmly in her throat, and began to talk.

'You don't understand. Rowler. He died weeks ago, and I... I never thought to... I didn't tell anyone because... because I... I...' Her resolve vanished as newly sharp images of Rowler's charred, broken form flooded her mind, and her courage deserted her. A heartsick wail escaped her lips and she collapsed into Zack, gripping onto his jacket for dear life, her lamentation redoubling as the full horror of what had happened came into sharp and unbearable focus.

Zack clasped her to him, gently stroking one hand through her hair, the other across her trembling back. 'Shh,' he breathed, trying to comfort and reassure her at the same time as attempting to make sense of what she had told him.

If Benjamin Rowler was indeed dead, and if it were true that his passing had occurred as far back as Layna said it had, that meant that his killers must feel that they had got away with it. Rage surged up inside him as the thought entered his brain, and in his mind's eye he saw vicious, conniving figures throwing back their heads and laughing at The Inside's security services – laughing at the dead man's memory. He thought of all the people that had phoned, each one yearning to discover what fate had befallen Benjamin and groaned involuntarily. How was he going to tell them?

'Zack?'

He looked round to see Samuel standing in the doorway, looking at him and Layna with a look of utmost bewilderment on his face.

'Layna? What's going on out here?' Samuel queried.

Instinctively, Zack's hand tightened protectively over that of his girlfriend, as his employer advanced upon them, his eyebrows raised.

Layna pressed herself into Zack, breathing in the wonderfully familiar scent that covered his t-shirt and bracing herself for the strike of the blow. She closed her eyes tightly, as if to shield herself from Brand, and concentrated on regulating her breathing and holding back the tears that still sparkled in her eyes, threatening to overflow. *Please don't make me answer,* she begged

Samuel silently, awfully aware of how futile her wishing was. *Please, please don't make me answer.*

Samuel was now standing directly in front of them and the quizzical expression had not faded from his face. 'Well?' he persisted, frowning.

Zack cleared his throat and locked his gaze with that of his boss. When he spoke, it was clear that he was struggling to keep his voice steady. 'He's dead, sir. Benjamin Rowler is dead.'

The effect of his words seemed to take place in slow motion. Samuel's eyes widened, his jaw tensed, and his stubby nails dug into his palms. His hands, which had been hanging in their natural, relaxed position at his sides less than thirty seconds ago, became fists that clenched so tightly that his knuckles were turning white. 'No,' he muttered, his mouth hanging open in disgust and astonishment. '*No!*'

Whimpering, Layna gnawed the corner of her bottom lip. 'It's… it's true,' she told Samuel in a quiet, unsteady voice. 'He's gone.' She broke off into another sob and buried her face in Zack's shirt, humiliated by the thought of what a sight she must look and guilt-ridden about the information she had been holding back from the government for so long. She clutched at him, trying to smother the wretched sounds that were now filling the air, one after the other, her face contorted with misery and despair. The feel of his body against hers both comforted and terrified her, for she could feel him shaking violently beside her, fighting to keep it together. 'Don't let go,' she pleaded, her voice now no louder than a raindrop on the pavement. 'Don't ever let me go.'

The pitiful begging seemed to shatter Zack's heart into a thousand tiny pieces. Lightly, he kissed the top of her head and murmured an equally slight-sounding reply. 'It's OK, my darling. I never will,' he whispered, so that only she could hear. 'I promise.'

Unmoved by the spectacle in front of him, Samuel cleared his throat and turned his hardened gaze upon Layna. 'How long have you known about this?'

There was a pause and then, reluctantly and with quaking hands, Layna released her hold upon Zack's t-shirt, though she was careful to grip his hand tightly at all times. She forced herself to look Samuel right in the eye. 'Since the day that it happened. It's... it's been... a while.' Feeling that her emotions were once again going to overcome her, she clasped her boyfriend's hand tighter than she ever had before and closed her eyes briefly before continuing, keeping her tone monotonous to avoid breaking down completely. 'He witnessed one of the FF's private meetings, and they abducted and tortured him. He... he's been dead for weeks.'

Determined to deny the evidence of his ears, Samuel started shaking his head repeatedly. 'But... but he can't be. He can't be... Dead for *weeks*? No, I refuse to believe it!' As if in an appeal for support, he glanced at Zack, his eyes imploring. 'It *can't* be true, can it?'

His clerk studied him very intensely for several moments and didn't break eye contact as he spoke in a voice that was strained but impressively level. 'I'm sorry, sir, but I trust Layna. I believe that what she's telling us is true.'

This was apparently too much for Samuel. His bloodshot eyes inflated to the size of golf balls and he let out a moan, which was quickly followed by words several octaves higher than his usual tone. 'My dear girl!' he yelped at Layna, '*why* did you let the FF do this? Surely, you realised at the time the sheer barbarism of what they were planning to do? Had you acted in some way to prevent this travesty from occurring, Rowler could still be alive today! Don't you see what you have *done*?' He broke off, his chest rising and falling with a speed that Zack had been certain up to this point was beyond human respiratory capabilities, the blood rushing past his ears like a herd of stampeding elephants. 'Can't you grasp the concept of an undercover operation?'

Cowering away from Brand's cold and ruthless words, Layna found that she was no longer able to control herself. Opening her mouth, she screamed like a grievously wounded child.

Zack was now solely responsible for bearing her body weight. Her tears soaked right through his clothes, her howls of desolation piercing him like the blade of a knife. Rage of a magnitude he had rarely experienced in his life erupted from deep inside him, and, before he could consider what he was about to say, words flew out of his mouth like a rain of bullets. 'It's not *her* fault!' he spat at his employer, his anger overtaking his rationality. '*She* didn't kill him!'

'Zack, don't you *understand?*' Samuel retorted, his voice too becoming suddenly amplified, 'Benjamin Rowler was viciously slaughtered by activists recruited by the Freedom Fighters terrorist group, the very organisation that Layna was hired to infiltrate! The reason she was placed in the FF as a mole was so that she could notify my government of any dangerous schemes the terrorists had hatched *before* they took place. Her performance has been lax from day one and, frankly, something like this was bound to happen! Had she done her job properly, Rowler and his family could have been placed into witness protection the instant he saw this "gathering" or whatever it was! He could've been saved! We could have... could have...' He trailed off, his anger fading as he saw clearly for the first time how his words were affecting the teenage girl, who was shaking uncontrollably before him. Thinking of his own daughter, who was only a few months older than Layna was now, he became instantly ensnared by shame. Slowly, he raised a hand to his sweat-dampened hair and pushed it out of his face. 'I'm sorry,' he told the couple stiffly. 'This is rather a big shock to me.'

Though Layna was still shell-shocked by his harsh words and hostile behaviour, she steadied herself and nodded her head slowly. 'I understand,' she replied softly.

Zack's expression remained cold and stiff. It was clear that he was barely restraining himself from voicing a comeback that was equally as cutting as the words Brand had been firing at Layna. The look of ill-disguised odium had not left Zack's eyes, but, thankfully, Samuel was too absorbed in his shock to notice.

Brand cleared his throat several times and swallowed loudly before he next addressed Layna. 'Where is the... the *body*?' As he spoke, what little colour his face had regained from his earlier outburst drained away into nothingness. He waited for her to respond, not by any means sure that he wanted to hear what she had to say.

She had known, of course, that the question would come and that she could not forever avoid voicing the terrible, insufferable truth that had plagued her conscience ever since those two fateful words had left Luke's mouth, so revoltingly casual and careless. Even so, in her desperation to shield herself – however ineffectively – from the unthinkable terror of what had become of Rowler's broken and mutilated form, she shook her head slowly. 'I... can't tell you.'

Revulsion filled Samuel's face in an instant, and he glared at her with narrowed eyes. 'What?' he spluttered. '*What*? Layna, Benjamin Rowler was a victim of a horrific crime, one that his family and friends must be informed of. They will be anxious to learn of his final resting place, wherever that may be. You are the only person that can aid them in the discovery of that information. Surely you can see the importance of this? They're frantic to find out more; they need to know.'

Zack fixed his employer with a steely glare. 'Sir, she's told you enough for now. You can see how much it's affecting her; it's tearing her up! Can't you just leave her alone?'

Samuel's caterpillar-like eyebrows arched in surprise. His employee's behaviour was usually nothing less than respectful, mature and perfectly pleasant; he never let his emotions get the better of him. This outburst was totally out of character.

Taking a step nearer, Zack opened his mouth in preparation for further protest, but Layna beat him to it.

Gently, she laid a hand on Zack's forearm. 'It's OK, baby,' she whispered.

They need to know. The words seemed to act as a needle, piercing the dense fog of fear and confusion in her brain, and she could now see clearly why Samuel had acted so vehemently. Rowler had not been a simple statistic or a mere pawn in the twisted chess game of the Freedom Fighters. He had been a real person, with his own life, his own emotions and his own loved ones. She thought of his bereft relatives, waiting on tenterhooks for something, *anything*, that could tell them more about what had happened to him. If she could give them that, surely the torture she put herself through in the name of her work could have some value, however small? Forcing herself to stare into the wild eyes of the ashen-faced Samuel, she shut out the graphic images bombarding her brain, and answered in as calm and collected a voice as she could muster. 'There is no body. It was set alight immediately after Rowler's murder. There's nothing left to bury.'

Letting out a long, low moan of paramount sorrow, Samuel took a step away from her and placed a hand to his temple, cursing repeatedly in dour undertones. Zack, meanwhile, stood his ground determinedly, providing the only sense of comfort and compassion in this nightmare. Layna looked at him and found the courage to remain on her feet, though every bone in her body seemed to cry out to her that she should fall to the ground and scream. If she could just hold on to him, she would be OK. If she could just hold on to him, she might just survive this.

'Can you give us a minute, please?' Zack asked coldly, regarding the man in front of him as though he were a stranger, his voice catching slightly in spite of his efforts to steady it, anger as well as sadness contributing to its shaky quality.

Samuel nodded curtly and, still muttering distractedly to himself, he left them in peace.

Immediately, Layna released the shriek of anguish she had been fighting to withhold from the world. Only the feel of Zack's arms around her and the regular, controlled rhythm of his breathing in her ears convinced her that she was still conscious, and that she had not slipped into some warped dream from which it was impossible to wake.

Closing her eyes, she whispered his name over and over again through her incessant tears, while he soothed her with continued consoling sentiments, gripping her tightly all the while.

'Oh baby,' he breathed, when at last the heart-wrenching sounds of her despair were hushed. 'I'm so, so sorry you had to go through that.'

Finally, Layna dashed a hand across her face to dry her eyes, regaining a small portion of her composure. 'Thanks, Zack' she sniffed.

'For what?' he asked dryly, his expression unexpectedly darkening along with his tone of voice. 'I did nothing; I just stood there and let him force you to tell him all that. I let him talk to you like you were some kind of Outsider criminal! I... I...' he broke off, rage preventing him from going any further. It was at that point, standing there drowning in his own outrage, that he realised that it was not directed at Samuel alone. The unprecedented amount of fury that was coursing through every inch of his body was not only aimed at the man who had inflicted Layna's terrible suffering, but also at the coward who had stood back and done nothing. Himself. 'I'm so, so sorry,' he repeated wretchedly. 'You deserve so much better.'

At this, Layna reached up and kissed him. That kiss told him a whole lot more than words ever could, and he did not pull back for a long time. When at last they had to break apart there was a glowing smile on Zack's face and the faintest traces of a rose-coloured blush upon his cheeks. It was the most endearing expression Layna had ever seen.

Looking into her strikingly intense eyes, Zack was overwhelmed by how much he cared for the beautiful, frightened and vulnerable angel he was now holding in his arms, and how far he was willing to go to protect her from harm. The smile on his face widened as he continued to look at her and slowly wipe away the last remnants of her tears. There was only one thing he could think of to say in such a situation – one thing that could at least go some way towards explaining how he felt about her. He had said it before, but he knew that now he meant it with all his heart and soul, with every fibre of his being.

'I love you, Layna,'

TWENTY-NINE

'What the hell happened to *you?*' demanded Bliss as, two days later, Liam sprinted across the playground towards her, Lucy, Nerris and Sherona, wearing a distinctly panicked expression. 'You look like someone's died or—'

'Is she following me?' Liam interrupted urgently, his eyes bulging so that he looked quite insane. *'Is she following me?'* He didn't wait for her to reply before diving between Lucy and Nerris, using them like some kind of human barricade.

Confused looks were exchanged between the four girls, and then Sherona turned to the still-hidden Liam and spoke as though comforting a frightened animal, 'Is *who* following you?'

Looking aghast at her lack of intuition, Liam answered in a voice that sounded like the hiss of a distressed and angry cat. 'Who d'you think?' he asked, crouching still lower so that nobody who didn't know what to look for would be able to see him, his eyes darting wildly back and forth.

As she realised what he was getting at, Bliss's eyes took on a depraved gleam. 'Jesus Christ, Liam, is Bamforth *still* stalking you?' She saw him nod and gave a snort of shameless laughter. 'After all this time? That's mental!'

'I only just managed to escape! I told her I needed to go to the loo, but I think she might have seen me coming over here!' He groaned loudly. 'You have to hide me!'

The all-too-obvious desperation in his voice made Lucy's heart lift slightly. 'So... you're definitely not interested then? In Bamforth, I mean?' she quizzed, speaking with an attempt at a casual air that did nothing to hide her elation from Nerris, Sherona and Bliss. 'You'd never, y'know, date her or something?'

Liam shook his head at once. 'Oh God, no; she really creeps me out!'

Instantaneously, a fire of triumph seemed to flare up in Lucy's stomach, and she replayed Liam's words in her head, a smile appearing on her face immediately. Her next thoughts were accompanied by the sound of a victory march. *He doesn't fancy her! He doesn't fancy her! He—*

'Lu?'

The sound of Liam's slow, concerned voice snapped her back to the real world and she looked hurriedly around at him, seeing that he'd risen to his feet. 'Yeah?' she asked.

'Are you OK? You look kind of... weird,' he stammered uncertainly. 'I mean, no offence, but...' he trailed off, shooting the others a look that all of them read to mean *'help me out here!'*

'You were blushing,' Nerris supplied, looking a little uncomfortable, 'and you went kind of… vacant.'

'No, I didn't!' she replied indignantly, feeling the colour in her face intensify considerably. 'Did I?'

'Well, we've been talking to you for the past five minutes with no response,' Sherona informed her, a knowing and evil grin now upon her face. 'So, either you're ignoring us…' She paused, her eyebrows slowly creeping skyward. 'Or you were distracted.'

Mortified, Lucy did her best to douse the bizarre internal flames that were now spreading rapidly through her insides, but it did no good. Instead, she searched madly for a change of subject, trying with all her might to avoid the gaze of the others as she did so.

For the first time in her life, she was grateful to Rebecca Bamforth, who appeared miraculously only a few metres away. Liam swore loudly, ducking once again out of sight. His friends hastily crowded around him, ensuring that he was completely obscured, just positioning themselves in time. Rebecca spotted them and pounced in the blink of an eye, trotting across to them at a surprisingly fast speed. 'Hi, guys!' she exclaimed, a little too brightly. 'I, like, sooo didn't see you there!'

Bliss elbowed Nerris hard in the ribs and nudged her forwards towards Bamforth. Being one of the most emotionally sensitive people she knew, Nerrisia seemed to Bliss to be the best equipped to deal with the situation.

Discreetly, Nerris threw her an atypically sour look and bit anxiously into the inside of her bottom lip, steeling herself before starting to speak. 'Er... hi, Rebecca' she began cautiously, 'How are you?'

'Oh, I'm totally cool,' she replied, peering round the side of the group and searching her surroundings like a human surveillance camera, rendering Liam paralysed with the fear she might discover him. 'Or, ya know, I will be when I find my Li Li.' She now tried and failed to appear laid-back as she asked, 'You peeps haven't seen him anywhere around, have ya?'

'Us? No, not since this morning, sorry,' Nerris stuttered, blushing.

The whole of Rebecca's make-up-smothered face sagged in disappointment.

Nerrisia found herself trying to console her. 'I think he might be upstairs in the art room if you wanna check there,' she improvised. 'He... umm... mentioned to me earlier that he had some work to catch up on up there.'

To her dismay, Rebecca shook her head. 'He's not there; I just checked.' Frowning slightly, she started to move closer, getting dangerously near to where Liam was concealed.

He held his breath and silently willed her to turn around, his heart sinking through the floor as the inevitability of his discovery and capture slowly dawned on him.

Once he was found, she was sure to imprison him in her company for as long as she possibly could; meaning, in turn, that he was not likely to escape her when the school day ended. If her previous behaviour was anything to go by, she was bound to have a last-minute homework issue and beg for help. He, as usual, would find himself unable to come up with a viable excuse not to assist her. This meant that, for a substantial amount of his time that evening, he would be trapped in her bedroom, fielding off questions that he really didn't want to answer; entirely at her mercy the whole time.

Wincing at the thought, he tried to shuffle round so that he was standing behind those of his friends whom Rebecca had already passed as she circled the group. Though he wanted nothing more than to simply run away as fast as his legs would carry him, the predicament with which he was now faced forced him to act without making sufficient noise or obvious enough movement to draw attention to himself. It was a near impossible task and one he knew that he had failed to execute successfully the instant he began to move.

Rebecca froze immediately and her expression changed to one tinted with suspicion. 'Did you guys, like, hear that?' she asked eagerly.

'Hear what?' asked Sherona, stamping surreptitiously on Liam's toe in punishment for his blunder – one that now appeared to be irreparable.

Barely stopping himself from crying out at the short, sharp pain, he had to content himself with looking daggers at the back of her head before returning to silent prayer, though he was now certain that praying was futile. In less than thirty seconds, he was surely doomed.

'Look, there he is!' cried a familiar voice, providing him with the tiniest glimmer of hope. 'Over there!'

'Where?' Rebecca demanded of the mystery speaker; the bizarre mix of aggression and excitement in her voice making Liam's insides writhe uncomfortably. '*Where?*'

'Over by that tree,' replied the first voice, 'but he's moving fast; you'd better get over there quick!'

No more needed to be said. After a pause no longer than a nanosecond, Liam could hear the sweet, sweet sound of Rebecca charging away at top speed; the noise she created resembling that of galloping horses.

'She's gone,' reported Bliss, as she turned to Liam.

He breathed a sigh of relief and pushed his way out of his human cage, his trademark easy-going grin back in place. 'Thanks guys,' he told them happily, 'you really saved my neck!'

'It was all down to Lu,' Nerrisia told him. 'We would've been scuppered back there if it weren't for her. That was some seriously quick thinking!'

Of course, Liam thought, a light bulb flickering on in his brain as he recognised that the voice he had heard moments before belonged to Lucy. 'Thanks,' he repeated, this time to her alone. 'That was great acting!'

She shrugged. 'No worries. We'd better get a move on though, before she twigs and comes back over.'

'Agreed,' Bliss said quickly, a grim expression crossing her face, 'I, for one, do *not* want to be here when she realises the friends of her Li Li told a lie lie!'

'Don't *ever* call me that again!' Liam ordered, while the others giggled appreciatively. '*D'you hear me?*'

Bliss's natural deviousness was once again apparent as she said, her eyes sparkling with a wicked glee, 'you try and stop me!'

THIRTY

'Thanks for letting me come up here late, miss.' Liam said, smiling at his music teacher Miss Butcher as they approached one of the school music rooms. 'I really appreciate it.'

'No problem,' she replied warmly, 'I wish all of my students were this enthusiastic to extend their learning. Are you sure you don't want to borrow one of the school guitars?'

'Oh, I'm sure.' Liam craned his neck to look affectionately at the black, canvas guitar case that was strung over his shoulder. 'I have to use my own or my creative processes would be disrupted.'

He said it so seriously that Miss Butcher couldn't help but laugh. 'OK. I'll be just down the corridor if you need me for anything. Don't forget to lock up when you're finished, will you?' she reminded him.

'I won't,' he promised. 'Bye, miss.'

His teacher set off briskly, and he entered the room, whistling merrily to himself.

He had two hours before his mother expected him home, and that meant he had ample time to work on his latest composition in peace before he was forced to return to the irritating whines of his twin siblings and the distracting cacophony that permeated his whole house. This was a rare and glorious opportunity, and one that he was determined to make the most of. Pulling the piano stool over to the small table in the corner, he gingerly unloaded his prize possession and began to expertly tune it up, his fingers performing the well-practised process almost automatically. When satisfied that the instrument was ready for use, he set it on the table and rummaged around in his school bag to find a small, blue notebook that was filled with handwritten lyrics.

Aside from his guitar, this was the only material item that Liam truly valued. Its contents represented everything he prized in life and taking a song from the page to the stage always felt brilliant. There was one creation he was currently working on that he was really looking forward to showing his bandmates: a romantic ballad that he was particularly proud of. It still needed a few tweaks, but he was confident that, with just a little more attention, it could be his best work yet. Finding the page in his book that bore the words and chords, Liam sat back in his chair and began to play.

It never failed to amaze him how quickly the magic of music could draw him in. At once, he became lost in his own world, no longer needing to refer to the book to know what he was doing. Closing his eyes, he listened as the song he was playing took him over. *There's nothing*, he thought with a contented sigh, *that compares to this*. The song was getting faster now, but he was unfazed and continued to play with a confidence that only a melody could bring him. Nothing could spoil this moment. Nothing.

'Li Li!' exclaimed a shrill, horribly recognisable voice, 'I, like, *reeeeally* hoped I'd run into you!'

Disbelief was the first sensation that flooded Liam's brain, followed by irritation and misery. How had she managed to find him? One hand curled protectively around the neck of his guitar, and he felt his teeth grind painfully together. Slowly, hardly daring to look in dread of what he'd see when he did, he opened his eyes. Sure enough, there she stood, one foot already over the threshold, her garish grin appearing to stretch her face to breaking point.

'Hi,' Liam squeaked, swallowing hard to moisten his throat, which had suddenly become as dry as sandpaper. 'I mean, hi, Becks! What're you... er... Why are you... I wasn't expecting to see you here.'

He could tell at once that she hadn't picked up the hesitancy in his voice, for her smile widened still more, and she walked, uninvited, into the room.

Moving faster than Liam had thought humanly possible, she had soon plonked herself next to him on the stool and put her arm around his shoulder. Hastily, he wriggled away from her touch, but she was not put off;

on the contrary, she seemed to take his displeasure for coyness, which only seemed to spur her on even further.

'Hey, it's all right,' she whispered, in what she clearly thought was a seductive tone, but that, in reality, made Liam want to vomit. 'We're both, like, total newbies at this.'

Edging still closer, she forced Liam to battle her for what tiny fraction of stool space remained unoccupied, so that he and his expensive guitar nearly toppled to the floor. Rebecca remained completely oblivious to his blatant unease and now turned her attention to the notebook, which still lay open in front of her. 'Ooooh!' she exclaimed eagerly, picking it up. 'What's this?'

'It's nothing,' he told her, frantically making a grab for it, 'it's just...'

Forced to break off, there was nothing he could do except watch in horror as she started to read his song, her heavily pencilled eyes widening as they took in every detail. The lyrics suddenly seemed unbelievably embarrassing, and Liam covered his face in despair. She was never going to let this drop and he knew it.

When she'd finished, her eyes were shining. 'It's, like, *reeeeally* good! Is it about... anyone you know?'

The suggestive purr that her voice had now adopted was terrifying to Liam, who was now searching desperately for an escape route. However, Rebecca had him pinned to the seat, and it was all he could do to tilt his neck far enough back to avoid a meeting between his lips and hers. He could feel his guitar slipping from his damp palm and his sense of panic was heightened right away. As Rebecca drew nearer, he clung to his most treasured possession as tightly as he could and forced his limbs into action, pulling himself away from her.

'I've... er....got to go. Sorry!' he gabbled, hurriedly snatching back the notebook, stuffing it into his bag and standing up before Bamforth could protest. 'See you around!' A surge of desperation sent him sprinting for the doorway, and he was within touching distance of his freedom when he felt Rebecca's hand on his sleeve. 'Where're you going?' she asked, pursing her lips and whining, 'I, like, only just got here!'

'Sorry!' Liam repeated – and he sprinted away from her as fast as he could.

*

It was only when he paused outside his front door to catch his breath that the full creepiness of what had just happened occurred to Liam. Bamforth had clearly tailed him all day in order to track him to the music room, and that meant she had seen everything he did. He shivered, disturbed greatly by the idea of someone spying on him like that. The others had been right all along; something had to be done to stop her. *But what*? he asked himself unhappily. *What can I do?*

However outrageous Bamforth's behaviour had been, he remained unwilling to subject her to the level of hostility that was sure to come her way if he disgraced her in public. Bliss would surely have a field day, and Rebecca would never recover from the humiliation of rejection. Shaking his head, Liam tried to formulate another solution, racking his brains for the easiest way to spare her feelings and yet break free of her advances. It was impossible. Each and every time he came into contact with her one on one, he couldn't get a word in edgeways, let alone get her to remain silent long enough for him to attempt to crush her hopes of any kind of relationship with him, while still remaining tactful. How on earth was he supposed to manage it?

His head spun with the hopelessness of the situation, and he found himself envying Zack for the first time since they'd met ten years ago. You didn't see him having this sort of girl trouble. In fact, you didn't see him having any girl trouble at all.

Liam sighed heavily and turned towards the house, deciding that comfort food was the only option here. *I'll sort it tomorrow,* he told himself. *How hard can it be?*

THIRTY-ONE

'Where've you been?' snapped Nick cantankerously, glaring at Delilah as she opened the door and entered his hotel room. 'You've been gone ages!'

'Down the pub,' she replied, eyebrows raised. 'Why?'

'In case you haven't noticed, there's work to be done here. We've got no hope of catching the mole if we've got agents vanishing left, right and centre!' Dragging a hand through his unkempt mane of hair, he exhaled loudly in frustration. 'Well?'

His dark mood didn't appear to faze her; in fact, she appeared lightly amused. 'What's got up your nose, huh?' she asked.

'What?'

'Don't try to kid me. It demeans you. Come on, out with it.'

Getting to his feet, Nick allowed himself an uncharacteristic smile. 'I could have you shot for the way you talk to me, Lieutenant Harper.'

'Yeah.' She nodded, laughing at his use of her official

title, her voice and her face cocky as a narcissistic comedian. 'But you won't, will you? You need me too much.'

'Need you? Hate to burst your bubble, Delilah, but I don't need anyone.'

'There you go again, talking crap. You need me 'cause I know you too well. I know too much. For instance, I know you're avoiding the question! What's up?'

'I told you, nothing. Look, I'm just tired all right? I'm stressed. I didn't mean to go off on you like that. I'm sorry.'

She snorted with laughter. 'Now I know something's wrong – you've never been that polite to me in your life! Sorry to disappoint you, pal, but the act isn't working.'

No sooner had Nick opened his mouth to protest once more that he was perfectly fine than his heart lurched terribly. Knight and Wafer had just walked into the room.

'Hi, you two,' Oliver began casually. 'What's going on?'

'Tell him that his little act isn't fooling anyone,' Delilah answered, gesturing to Nick and rolling her eyes. 'You've noticed he's hiding something, right?'

Luke advanced at a leisurely pace, one that would arouse unease in nobody but Nick. Malice lit up his permanently icy eyes, and he allowed himself a tiny smile. 'Hiding something?' he purred. 'Like what?'

He was now close enough that, had he wanted to, he could have grasped Nick by the shoulder and held him where he stood. Instead, Luke chose to rely on the other man's fear to lock him in place – a highly effective strategy.

Cookson stood helpless beside him, unable to move an inch, feeling as though he were choking on his own terror. This was a clever and devious test of his nerve. The logical thing to do would, of course, be to reveal Luke and Oliver's scheme to Delilah, and attempt to regain control of the situation with her assistance, which may at least be marginally possible, if a little risky. *Yes,* he decided, emboldened by the prospect of outing his two enemies as traitors, *that's simple enough; I can do that.* He opened his mouth to speak, but something stopped him in his tracks.

Oliver's cough was quiet and discreet, and on any other day may have seemed completely natural. However, Nick's senses had been sent into overdrive by the threat of Luke in such close proximity, and his eyes darted to where the sound had come from, like a pair of trapped flies attempting to evade human capture. It was with a thrill of sheer terror that he saw Oliver's eyes were trained on Luke's belt.

'Look,' Wafer mouthed, glancing up quickly and seeing that he had succeeded in catching Nick's attention. His hard gaze developed a new air of bone-chilling satisfaction.

Fearful of what he might see, but completely terrified of what might happen behind his back if he did not look, Nick obeyed the order hesitantly and barely stopped himself retching at what his eyes encountered.

There it was, the one thing that could render his rational action plan useless: a small, silver-and-black pistol, upon which Luke's hand now rested. Nick's own gun currently resided in his trouser pocket, and – when it came to drawing weapons – he was fast, but everyone in the room knew that Luke was faster. Smugly, Knight stroked his deathly white index finger over the firearm and waited for Nick's spirit to fail him. As expected, the wait was transitory.

'See? They didn't notice anything,' Nick croaked, turning to Delilah and trying desperately to feign a laid-back, relaxed manner, 'I'm fine.'

It did not take a genius to see that she wasn't fooled, but – mercifully for him – she let the matter drop for the time being, though anyone who knew her at all knew that she would not forget about it entirely. She shrugged. 'OK. Have any of you seen Layna? We were planning to sneak over the border to The Inside and stake out Samuel Brand's place; see if any of those MPs visit during the day. You know, to gather intelligence.'

'She left around an hour ago,' Nick replied, glad that the focus had now shifted away from him. 'Said she wanted to check something out first.'

Intrigued, Delilah nodded. 'OK, guess I'd better go and catch her up then. See ya.' She pulled the hood of her jacket up and headed for the door but was prevented from leaving by Wafer.

'Can I come too?' he asked, 'I've nothing to do back here.'

'If that's all right with Nick,' she answered, 'and if you don't wreck the whole thing, then yeah, I s'pose so.'

Luke turned to Nick, one hand still in contact with the gun that held all the power. 'That's fine, right, mate?' Knight asked, the danger in his voice subtle and all the more hostile for it.

'Sure,' Nick agreed hastily. 'Whatever. We can hold things down here for a while.'

'Excellent,' Oliver grinned, his gaze meeting Luke's for a single moment, 'C'mon, Delilah.'

They left and panic enveloped Nick in an instant. He was now alone in a room with an armed and ruthless opponent, and there was, as far as he could see, no escape. Oh why hadn't he stopped Delilah, his one definite ally in these inconceivably perilous times, leaving him unprotected? Shamed by the thought that he needed protection from anyone, least of all from his female second in command, he forced himself to face Knight with insincere confidence. 'Piss off, Luke. Now.'

'Oh, fancy ourselves the boss, do we? I shall have to practise my bowing technique,' Luke mocked. 'In your dreams, Cookson.'

'I said, piss off! I'm the commander here, got it?'

'That's as may be, but I'm the fighter, I'm the survivor and the brave heart. I'm the one who could shoot you dead – right here, right now. Oh, by all means pull out your gun, we both know you'd never have the guts to use it. We both know I'm trigger-happy. We both know I could kill you before you'd even drawn the thing.' Unhurriedly, he pulled the shooter from his belt and pointed it directly at Nick's heart.

Frantic for a way out, Nick racked his brains for something, anything, that could prevent Luke from killing him. For, no matter what he said to the contrary, Knight held control of this situation, and there was nothing Nick could say or do to change that. The pistol was still pointing forwards, Luke's arm remarkably steady given what he was about to do. In fact, it was rigid as an iron pole. This was to be a remarkably calm murder.

It was then that it hit Nick. If he were going to die, he would be cold on the floor by now, Luke having already committed the crime that was second nature to him. Nick was still alive. This meant that he was not going to be murdered today. 'Why haven't you done it?' he spat, his eyes narrowing in contempt. 'If you were going to do it, I wouldn't still be standing here, would I?'

'Worked that one out, have you? Took you long enough.' He laughed coldly. 'I meant what I said, I *could* kill you, but I won't – not yet. Not now.'

'And why's that?' Though he tried to keep his tone stony and unreceptive, Nick could not fully purge his voice of the confusion he felt at this unexpected turn of events. 'Why deprive yourself of the pleasure?'

Another humourless laugh preceded Luke's next words, and Nick felt his heart racing as he waited to discover what the answer would be. He could not for the life of him anticipate what kept Knight from pulling the trigger, but it was important, whatever it was – vital, in fact – that Nick heard it. Whatever its nature, it was the only thing that stood between him and imminent mortality, and if this seemingly unstoppable foe had a weakness, Nick was determined to grasp it with both hands. It wasn't long before Luke provided him with the information he craved so badly, but the effect was a level of horror unprecedented to Nicholas Cookson.

Luke smiled maliciously and said, in a voice that leached any remaining hope from Nick's soul. 'It'd make things too easy for you.'

'What… what are you talking about?' he stammered, his voice catching as his dread threatened to overwhelm him, his breathing becoming sharp and difficult. The pretence of courage gone for good, his whole body began shaking with fright. 'What d'you mean?'

Again, Luke let out a cold guffaw of triumph. 'I confess, I enjoy our little mind games. They provide me with a pleasant sideshow as I plan your breakdown. Gives me confirmation, if any were needed, that you cannot and will not fight back. A broken enemy is easier to destroy than a spirited one, you see. Rest assured – my pathetic, little friend – I am going to break you. Piece by piece, bit by bit, until there's nothing left to take. Then, and only then, I'll pull the trigger, understand? I look forward to next time.'

THIRTY-TWO

The plans were made – the trap set. Everyone involved was in position, and there was nothing to do now but wait for the chance to put into practice the plan that had taken so long to put together. The wait was agony.

Layna was sitting upon the velvet-covered seat beside Samuel's front door, watching his garden through a miniscule gap in the curtain. Anxiously, she toyed with one of the tassels sewn onto her perch, repeatedly twisting it into knots and unravelling it again. She wasn't at all sure she was ready for this.

'How are you holding up?' asked a voice from behind her.

It was gentle, but she was so on edge that it made her start.

Zack, the speaker, felt a surge of guilt. 'Sorry,' he apologised, 'I guess not too well?'

'Don't worry, I'm fine.' She gave a laugh that was much too high to be natural. 'Just a little nervous. I just need a moment, you know, before I…' she broke off, nibbling the fingernails on her left hand, the way she always did when she was worried.

He sighed and sat down beside her, holding out a steaming, white mug. 'Tea,' he explained. 'Take the edge off a bit.'

Taking it, Layna smiled. 'I thought that was alcohol?'

He nodded, laughing too. 'Best I could do, I'm afraid,' he sighed. 'We *are* underage, and my boss is down the hall. I'm not exactly in his good books after what happened the other day, and he's kind of tetchy about all this going on so close to his house. Lucy's with him and her mum in the living room; they're trying to chill him out a bit, but I don't reckon it's gonna work. I don't know what he's uptight about, though; it's *you* who's putting your neck on the line. It's *you* who should be...' He stopped at the expression on her face and turned as red as a roaring fire. 'Oh God, sorry. I'm not being much help am I?'

'Doesn't matter; you cheered me up just being here. It makes me feel better about everything, about this.' She blushed royally. 'That sounded so cheesy! I just meant to be romantic.'

'I suppose both of us need practice at that,' he replied, grinning and shuffling closer to her, 'and we might as well start now.' He leaned in to kiss her – a glint in his eye.

'Zack, *no*,' she protested, though her laughter made it difficult for her to sound severe. 'You'll make me spill this everywhere! Besides, people are staring!'

It was true; several of those nearest to them, including numerous uniformed police officers and security men, had now focused their attention upon the pair. Several were nudging each other and chuckling. Despite their relaxed façade, Zack could see that many of them looked just as pale and nervy as Layna had a few minutes earlier, and it pulled his mind back to the matter in hand.

'Shouldn't you be waiting out there?' he asked as he moved back, his expression serious once more.

'I'm waiting for a signal from PC Timmons,' Layna explained. 'She's in charge here.'

'Really?' Zack frowned, 'This is a bit of an advanced job for a PC isn't it?' Having remained bitter towards Timmons after what had happened after the Closes' rescue, he was not at all thrilled by the idea of anyone he cared about taking orders from her, least of all Layna.

'I'll be OK,' she murmured, placing a hand reassuringly on his forearm.

'I don't want you going out there by yourself,' he told her firmly, 'It's way too dangerous.'

'I've got my bulletproof gear on' she reminded him 'and as soon as I give the signal, armed backup will be there. I'll be perfectly safe. So, have your friends come over for moral support?'

The change of subject was blatantly obvious and sounded jarring in the conversation, but he was grateful for it all the same and latched onto it immediately. 'Yeah, they're around here somewhere, along with half The Inside by the looks of things. This place is packed out; it's crazy isn't it?'

The building, though huge by any usual standards, appeared to have shrunk to the size of a dolls' house on account of the thrumming crowd now within its walls. Apart from various members of the police force, government officials and additional security personnel, numerous members of the public – who had no clear reason to be there – crowded each and every room, making the place feel unbearably enclosed. Zack hoped sincerely that none of the assembled mob suffered from claustrophobia, as that would create unnecessary drama in the midst of a situation that was already proving painfully difficult to control. He turned back to Layna, unwilling to allow his mind to picture all the possible disasters that could occur in such cramped conditions.

'You know,' he said wistfully, 'in the Old World, when there wasn't an Inside or Outside, they actually had separate buildings for government meetings and the like, not everything taking place in the prime minister's house. I mean, they had a few meetings there, but mostly they had big fancy offices. That would certainly make things easier, wouldn't it? There's not enough space in here to swing a kitten!'

She laughed. 'How do you know so much about the past? You don't go to school or anything, so when d'you find the time to study it?'

'I dunno; I just love to read. We can learn a lot from the past, or so they say. I haven't learned anything yet and no one else seems to care about history.' He slipped his arm carefully around her shoulders. 'You'll get used to my weirdness,' he told her with a slightly embarrassed smile.

'What weirdness, genius?' she asked, reaching up to peck him on the cheek and leaning against him contentedly.

He felt his heart flutter, like the first butterfly of summer, and a warm rush of affection swept over him as he looked at her. 'Thanks.'

At that moment, PC Timmons strode over to them, a somewhat stony expression on her face. 'Hello, you two,' she greeted them, her lips pursed in disapproval, 'It's a pleasure to see you again.'

She was a terrible liar, and Zack did not bother to return her hollow compliment. Instead, he gave her a questioning look, prompting her to get to the point.

She seemed to pick up on his intention and cleared her throat importantly. 'Miss Johns,' she announced, 'we are all set to go here so, if you would come with me, we can do a final security check.' She looked at Layna expectantly, giving Zack not even the merest of glances before starting to walk away.

Layna looked at her boyfriend apologetically and opened her mouth to protest at PC Timmons's behaviour, but Zack shook his head quickly. Keeping his eyes on the policewoman's back, he rose purposefully to his feet.

Timmons turned sharply and fixed him with an unpleasant stare. 'What're you doing?'

'She's not going anywhere without me, got it?' he told her, 'This girl is everything to me, and, if you don't mind me saying, you haven't exactly proven yourself capable of looking after her!' The venom within his voice became all the more apparent as he hissed out his next words, 'I haven't forgotten what happened last time, Officer.' Slowly and deliberately, he made his hand into a claw and drew it across his cheek, his expression hateful and unforgiving.

PC Timmons winced involuntarily and her face paled considerably. 'Very well,' she snapped, flustered, 'but you do not leave this building!'

Zack nodded tightly. 'Agreed,' he consented sombrely 'For her sake, not yours.'

There was a moment of icy coldness between them, and then Layna tentatively reached forwards and squeezed Zack's hand lightly with her own. Instantly, he felt his whole body fill once again with the delicious warmth he had felt before PC Timmons had appeared. Layna was the important one here – the only one that truly had a reason to complain – and yet here she was as calm as still, sunlit water.

Taking a deep breath, he looked at her and smiled. 'Time to do this' he whispered, speaking for her ears alone this time.

She only nodded, suddenly unable to form words.

Her clothes had already been wired up with a discreetly placed microphone and, as she had already assured Zack, nearly everything she was wearing was bulletproof. She was one hundred per cent safe. So, why had a vice-like hand of iron suddenly clamped itself around her chest, ruthlessly preventing her from drawing breath? Why did she find herself overcome with an almost unbearable desire to beg them all not to force her into this?

Why me? she thought miserably, a lump rising swiftly and unexpectedly in her throat, *Why does it have to be me?*

Though she tried to force herself to think of the greater good and the colossal impact her actions had the potential to have on The Inside's future, the only thing she could see, at this moment, was the terrifying situation she was mere moments away from being thrown into. How was it that she now shouldered such a gigantic responsibility? What had possessed her to take the position of mole in the first place? Was it really too late to back out?

Sickness swelled in her stomach as all these questions and more swirled around her mind, each one becoming jumbled with those that had preceded it, until she could barely manage to continue placing one foot in front of the other. It seemed to her that – no matter how far she walked – the back door was getting further and further away, not closer. It was, therefore, a great surprise to find herself suddenly hearing PC Timmons briefing her about how best to ensure her own safety and reminding her how proceedings were supposed to unfold.

'You will slip out of the building via this rear entrance and assume your position at the surveillance point prearranged with the Freedom Fighter agent you are due to meet, all the while making sure that you are not seen.' Timmons glanced apprehensively over her shoulder, betraying with that unconscious gesture that she was not as collected as she appeared. 'When your target arrives, keep them talking for as long as possible, discussing their involvement with the FF in particular. If you require assistance or feel you have gathered sufficient evidence to secure a prosecution, run your left hand through your hair, understand?'

Nodding slowly, Layna struggled to speak through her anxiety. 'She'll be armed,' she warned, 'The FF agent, I mean.'

Timmons's eyes became icier still and, when she spoke, her voice was deadly serious. 'So will we, Miss Johns; so will we.'

THIRTY-THREE

'Is it just me or does something not feel right about this?' Oliver asked as he and Delilah made their way towards Samuel Brand's house, continuously glancing over their shoulders as they went.

'What are you on about?' asked Delilah irritably, not looking at him.

Oliver shrugged. 'I dunno; this is important, and I want everything to go right. Maybe I'm just being paranoid or something but—'

'Shh!' his colleague interrupted quickly, her voice taking on a new urgency. 'D'you want the whole place to hear us?'

'Sorry,' replied Wafer, looking guilty, 'I'm just edgy, that's all.'

'I knew it was a mistake taking you with me,' she grumbled darkly, annoyance permeating her tone, 'I'm gonna kill Nick for agreeing when we get back!'

Her words gave Oliver an idea; if he was truly to overthrow the Commander, then he was going to have to find out as much as possible about him. Who better to supply him with the necessary information than Cookson's unsuspecting best friend? Smiling slyly to himself, he feigned innocent curiosity. 'You and he grew up together, right?' he probed experimentally.

'Yeah, but what's it to you?'

'Nothing; I just wondered. Were you two close back then?'

'None of your business!' Harper told him, her tone becoming defensive 'Quit the interrogation already; I'm not some Insider you're holding prisoner!'

'Jeez, chill out! Rich of you to tell me to be quiet, you're screaming like a bloody banshee!'

She turned to glare at him reproachfully. 'I can always send you back, ya know, and you'd be making your way to base by yourself, without anyone to watch your back. So unless you fancy a one-way trip to a top-security prison cell, I'd advise you to shut your trap!'

Oliver rolled his eyes in a melodramatic fashion, and his eyebrows edged several inches skyward, but he didn't dare question her about Nick any further.

They walked the rest of the way in silence.

↗

By the time they found Layna, now concealed in the trees that lined the expanse opposite the Brands' house with a stolen camera around her neck, Oliver and Delilah were neglecting even to make eye contact with each other.

Immediately, Delilah launched into a fiery monologue of griping, and, though all of it was whispered, it had as much fury in it as the loudest rant. 'He's gonna be the death of us, you mark my words! You'd think he was a flippin' elephant, the noise he made! I swear, the Insider cops must all be deaf or something; we should both be banged up by now!'

'And you're complaining that you're not?' Layna queried, her expression slightly mocking. 'Come and give me a hand will you? I've been waiting for ages!'

Harper nodded and moved over to crouch beside her. 'Got anything good yet?' she demanded.

With a sigh, Layna shook her head. 'Nobody's been in or out since I got here, and the only car on the drive is his. Wherever the government do meet, it isn't here. All I've been able to do is photograph the house, and a fat lot of good that'll do us. Afraid you two might've had a wasted trip.' Her gaze moved over to Oliver, who was unloading his equipment a short distance away. 'I didn't realise he would be here.'

'Believe me,' Delilah replied with a wry smile, 'I wish he wasn't.'

The unexpected appearance of Wafer, one of Benjamin Rowler's brutal killers, added a whole new dimension to the undercover operation that was about to unfold. The arrest that had been planned was that of Delilah Harper, on a charge of Freedom Fighter membership; it had not for a second crossed anybody's mind that she may bring company. Once again, thoughts of Rowler's grief-stricken friends and family materialised at the forefront of Layna's mind, rapidly followed by an unsettling sensation of sick anticipation. At last, she could begin to make amends for the terrible and cowardly mistake she had made in not confessing her knowledge of Benjamin's death until the suffering of his loved ones had become excruciatingly intense. Now was the moment to attempt to make things better. Now was the moment to step up to the plate.

Taking a deep breath, she pondered how best to hint to those within the house that the man they were now watching was a murderer. Choosing her words with utmost care, she tried her best to make her voice sound at ease. 'Where d'you suppose he and Luke took Rowler's body before they, you know... did what they did to it?' she asked. Despite her relaxed façade, the last few words caught in her throat. *Keep your head, Layna*, she told herself. *Don't blow it now.*

Delilah was silent as she considered the question, sighing heavily before responding. 'Been thinking about it a lot, huh?' she asked grimly.

All Layna could do was jerk her head in confirmation.

Sighing again, Harper nodded slowly. 'Just like me,' she said softly, her back turned.

Her tone and words sent a flicker of surprise through Layna's body. Though she was unsure of the reply she had been expecting, the one she had just received had caught her well and truly off guard. 'What d'you mean?'

There was another pause, and then Delilah sighed deeply for a third time. Though Layna could not see it, her eyes took on a haunted look as she answered. 'I'm a Freedom Fighter Layna. That means I've done things I'm not proud of. It doesn't make me heartless.'

'I didn't say that…'

'You didn't have to say it; your tone said everything for you. I know how I must seem…how I must look to you. When I joined the FF, I would've been disgusted by me too, but we just have to get on with things, OK? Just do what has to be done and be who we have to be. That's the life we lead. Sometimes, we just have to move on.'

Her voice carried an unambiguous finality, and Layna realised that to press her further would be dangerous, yet she couldn't help asking just one more thing.

'How do you move on, Delilah?' she whispered, thoroughly unprepared for how quiet and shaky the words sounded. Sniffing loudly and clearing her throat, she tried to cover her emotion before either one of the FF agents picked up on it. Fortunately, Oliver was entirely focused on taking snapshots and had selected a vantage point from which to procure his images that was a good distance out of earshot, while Delilah appeared locked in her own mind.

Ordering herself not to let her composure drop again, Layna aimed her camera at the building once more and busied herself with snapping photos. It would soon be time to give Timmons and the others the signal to move in for the ambush, but it was essential that the moment of attack was chosen with paramount care. *You only get one shot at this,* she reminded herself as she continued her work. *Don't blow it.*

Adrenalin pumped through her veins, and her heart pounded like a war drum. She fought to appear calm and collected on the surface, while preparing herself internally for her next move. Steadying her nerves with a single deep breath, Layna slowly raised her left hand. Dreadfully aware of how much it was shaking, she touched it to her head and combed her fingers through her hair, doing her best to make the gesture appear ordinary and natural.

All she could do now was wait.

The speed with which the following events unfolded was unbelievable. Instantaneously, six burly Inside policemen charged towards them, moving with an agility that was paradoxical to their muscular builds. Delilah swore savagely and abandoned her apparatus. She was immediately alert. Oliver whipped his handgun from his pocket and prepared to fight. Without warning, the Insiders opened fire on the activists.

'Shit!' Harper exclaimed, ducking out of range, her own instinct being to make an escape as opposed to retaliating. 'Shit, shit, *shit!*'

Wafer was now firing back at the armed men, who were advancing with still more speed and aggression, and the shoot-out was escalating into all out warfare. Bullets flew towards them like driving rain, and both Layna and Delilah were forced to their knees in self-preservation.

'C'mon!' Delilah bellowed, looking up at Oliver, who had just shot one of the Insiders through the leg. She glared at him, her eyes burning with urgency. 'We have to get out of here; there's too many of them!'

Oliver ignored her. He was shouting and swearing at the police for all he was worth, all the while continuing to shoot at them. Two of the officers had battled their way towards him, and he was now struggling ferociously against them, while a colleague of theirs informed him that he was under arrest. He hurled abuse at them at the top of his lungs, but it was clear that he had no chance of escape.

'C'mon,' Delilah urged again, this time directing her speech at Layna. 'Let's go.' Spotting the torn expression on Layna's face, Delilah started to tug at her arm, 'Here's a lesson in Freedom Fighter survival: when push comes to shove, you look out for yourself.'

Unbeknownst to her co-worker, it was not thoughts of Oliver that held Layna on the spot, but the image of Zack – still waiting inside the house – whom she knew would be a nervous wreck if she did not return. *But surely,* she thought, *he knew I'd have to leave with the FF? Surely he understood that?* Yet, as she looked at the still-struggling law enforcement squad, a terrible realisation seemed to hit her square in the chest: Zack was expecting the Freedom Fighters to be arrested, and thus expecting Layna to come back. However, it was clear that this part of the initiative hadn't gone to plan. Delilah was going to get away, and it would be detrimental to Layna's own survival not to follow. The words Harper had just uttered were proof enough that she didn't believe in emotional attachments, and if Layna hesitated for too long, there was a real possibility that her true motives would be exposed.

Thinking regretfully of her anxious boyfriend for a second longer, Layna allowed herself to be pulled away.

THIRTY-FOUR

By the following week, the whole world seemed to know that Oliver Wafer had been arrested and charged with Rowler's murder, as well as those of eight other Inside civilians and three government officials. He had also received a charge of grievous bodily harm and an additional one for seven years of FF membership. His image was ever-present on every TV channel going, as well as in many big-time newspapers. At last, it appeared that Samuel Brand's parliament was not a total write-off, and everybody close to him was immensely relieved.

The public, who seemed satisfied with the constant news updates now readily available to them, had finally relented in their letter writing, therefore affording Zack valuable time with his friends. Given how rare this had been lately, it seemed heavenly to him. His happiness rubbed off on the others, and it wasn't long until the pressures of recent times were all but forgotten.

There was only one major problem that remained

to cast a shadow over their day to day lives: the fact that Rebecca was still refusing to back away from Liam.

Due to the dramatic events that had taken place since she had cornered him in the music room, Liam had yet to confront Bamforth about how her advances were making him feel. Subsequently, she was continuing to tail him like a shadow, completely humiliating him with her cringeworthy remarks and painfully unsubtle flirtations. Apart from Lucy, his friends found the whole thing hilarious and forever seemed to be teasing him about it. Despite how unhappy the situation was rendering him, he remained insistent that he would not have it out with Bamforth in front of anybody else, no matter how much the others tried to pressure him into putting the situation to rest. 'I'll sort it' he told them repeatedly, 'I just need to pick my moment.'

Though they were all growing increasingly exasperated with the matter, his friends were too busy enjoying the relative peace that had settled over their lives to think about it too much, so they let things lie for quite some time. In fact, the situation remained unchanged, until Liam was faced with a wake-up call.

He was lounging around beneath the friends' school tree, accompanied by the girls and checking to see that Rebecca wasn't lurking about anywhere, when a harassed looking Miss Butcher came bustling over, her expression severe.

'Liam, I have been looking all over for you!' she announced, 'I need a word!'

'Yes, miss?' he asked, getting to his feet and shooting his mates a confused look. 'How can I help you?'

The frown on his teacher's face became yet more serious. 'Given what you and your friends witnessed not long ago, I've tried to put it off for as long as I can, but I'm afraid I can't let you off the hook any longer!' she told him, her voice rising to a shrill squeal as she spoke.

'I don't under—' Liam began, his stomach clenching with anxiety and foreboding.

But Miss Butcher waved an impatient hand to silence him and ploughed on. 'When I offered you my room to practise in you promised me that you would lock the door. How do you suppose I felt when I came up there the next morning and found that the door was wide open?' She clicked her tongue impatiently and fixed him with an accusing stare.

Liam felt his heart plummet to the floor. 'The door,' he muttered, clapping a hand to his forehead, 'I completely forgot!'

'Mmm,' she murmured, nodding slowly and folding her arms. 'You did. And because you "completely forgot", a very expensive piano was left exposed all night long! What have you got to say for yourself?' She sighed deeply, her expression changing to one of huge disappointment. 'I thought I could rely on you.'

Face burning, eyes firmly fixated upon the newly cut grass below him, Liam gave an unintelligible apology, his voice trailing off into nothing long before he had finished.

Miss Butcher looked at him in disapproval. 'I hope you weren't planning on coming up there again because henceforth you're banned until further notice, understand? I expected better from you, Liam.'

'I... sorry, Miss Butcher,' he stammered.

'Quite. Now I've got some things to sort out, and, frankly, I haven't got the time to waste on punishing you further, so consider yourself lucky!'

'Yes, miss,' he mumbled miserably.

Giving him a brisk nod, she strode away without another word, leaving the group of friends feeling immensely awkward.

'Feeling up to explaining any of that?' Bliss asked after a while.

Liam's shoulders slumped, and he shot her a desperately morose look. 'Take a wild guess!'

At once, Bliss leapt in with the usual spiel given after even the vaguest mention of Rebecca. 'You've gotta stop her ruining your life like this!' she told him, 'It's getting out of control!'

'I know but—

'No buts!' she snapped, stamping her foot in annoyance. 'You *have* to do something about her!' Fearing that the severity of the situation had still not got through to him, she looked round at the others for support. 'Right, guys?'

'Definitely,' Lucy answered, nodding her head just a fraction too vigorously.

Sherona, Nerris and Bliss all smirked knowingly at her, and her cheeks turned peony pink.

'For… for your sake, I mean,' she stammered, avoiding everyone's gaze.

Staggeringly, Liam appeared to have overlooked her strange behaviour yet again – too preoccupied with his anxieties about Bamforth to pay his friend that much attention. 'I just hate the idea of letting her down,' he explained. 'I couldn't do it in front of everyone; she'd be mortified!'

'And? She's been embarrassing *you* for months!' Bliss pointed out. 'It's all getting beyond a joke now. If you'd taken my advice to begin with, you'd still be Butcher's little pet.'

Liam's embarrassment escalated at her words for, however much he was loath to admit it, he could see that she was right. 'Whatever,' he muttered. 'Can we move on, please?'

Nerris, feeling that her friend had suffered quite enough for one lunchtime, nodded and cast around for something to say that would steer the conversation in a new and less personal direction. Struck by sudden inspiration, she turned to Lucy, who was also looking very awkward, and said, 'I wonder what Zack's up to? With all the stuff on the news lately, I shouldn't think he's got much to do at your place.'

Lucy raised her eyebrows and laughed dryly. 'That Mrs Pollington must've thought the same thing, 'cause she's taken to phoning him up all the time to complain. I dunno how he's being so civil to her; if it were me, I'd have told her to shove it where the sun don't shine long before now!'

'Isn't she the one who pestered him the most over the Outsiders?' Nerris asked, her face creasing up slightly in confusion. 'The police have got one of them now, and it's probably only the beginning. What's to complain about?'

Pulling a bemused and yet comical face, Lucy chuckled before answering. 'Anything. Taxes, the weather, retirement homes – everything and anything! It's driving *me* crazy, let alone him! Still, he doesn't seem too bothered by it. Personally, I think Pollington needs her head checked out.'

While Sherona, Bliss and Liam each voiced their agreement, Nerris attempted, as usual, to see the situation from everybody's perspective. 'Maybe she's lonely,' she suggested, her voice becoming concerned, and she chewed anxiously at her nails. 'I mean, if she lives all by herself without anyone to talk to, she might just be—'

'Oh, give me strength!' Bliss interrupted, swapping exasperated looks with the others before turning to Nerris, and rolling her eyes with a mixture of vexation and amusement. 'Will you *ever* stop being weird? You and Liam are as bad as each other when it comes to spotting a freak, even when they're staring you right in the face! The pair of you are just too...'

'Nice?' Liam asked. 'That particular quality seems a bit of a foreign concept to you!' He gave her a dig in the ribs, startling her and making her shriek in angry protest.

'Get off!' she told him fiercely. 'And I *am* nice!' When the expected support of the others didn't come, Bliss shoved Liam away from her and turned her wrath upon them instead. 'Hey, you lot, help me out here!'

Still, the others gave no response except a mischievous, pointed look.

In mock outrage, Bliss opened her mouth to shoot them a fiery retort, but was halted in her tracks by the high-pitched screech of the school bell. Amidst the cacophonous thunderstorm of noise that greeted this rallying call, she and her friends leapt to their feet and quickly became lost in the crowd of students now gravitating towards the main Inside High building.

Despite the looming prospect of the drab and lengthy double science class that now lay ahead of him, Liam felt a surge of happiness as he relived the hilarious expression on Bliss's face when the others had failed to come to her defence. Grinning cheerfully to himself, he continued walking with a spring in his step, in spite of the fact that he was being continually jostled by the limbs and bags of his stampeding classmates.

He was so lacking in concentration that he collided headlong with Jake, who gave a cry of surprise and barely stopped himself falling over.

'Jeez, mate!' Jake exclaimed. 'Watch it!'

'Sorry,' Liam apologised, 'I was distracted.'

Jake shrugged. 'It's OK, nothing's broken. By the way, Rebecca Bamforth's looking for some guy she called Li

Li, and I reckon she means you. Bit of a dodgy nickname though, if you ask me.' Noticing the expression on Liam's face, he chortled. 'I feel for you mate,' he said and pressed forwards into the tumult.

A sudden coldness had descended over Liam, and he felt the bubble of happiness inside him burst as though pierced by a needle of despair at the thought of what he had to do after school. Even the thought of Rebecca's face when he told her he wasn't interested in a relationship made him want to turn and run, but this time he knew he had to bite the bullet and get the confrontation over with. Backing out now was not an option. This had gone far enough.

THIRTY-FIVE

'Are you even listening to me?' Nerris asked later that afternoon as she looked up from filling in the results table she had drawn in her science book to see that Liam, her chosen partner for that day's experiment, was gazing at the clock on the wall with a crestfallen expression that was most unlike him. 'You've not said a word for ages.'

'Hmm?' he muttered vaguely, his eyes flickering to her for half a second before returning to the classroom wall, 'What did you say?'

Irritation flooded through her at once, and she folded her arms, glaring at the back of his head. 'I knew you weren't paying attention!' she fumed, 'I've been trying to explain all our results to you for the past forty minutes, and you've completely ignored… oh, for goodness sake!' For all the impression her words were making on him, she may as well have been talking to the desk.

Liam had sunk back into his stupor, and his brain seemed incapable of registering anything but the faint ticking of the clock in which he was absorbed. Noticing this, Nerris gave up and slammed the cover of her book shut. Even the slightest hope of getting through to him at any point during the remainder of this lesson was optimistic to the point of idiocy, and she was not about to waste any more breath attempting it.

Of course, there were no prizes for guessing the reason behind Liam's unfocused state of mind. The end of the day was fast approaching, and that meant that the time would soon come for Liam's conversation with Rebecca. From Liam's point of view, this meant that his time for thinking up an appropriate way to explain things to his fervent admirer was quickly running out.

Though she sympathised with his predicament, Nerris was growing increasingly irritated by his behaviour, and was now struggling to remain calm and collected. Sitting back in her chair, she watched enviously as, a few tables in front of her, Lucy and Sherona launched into an animated discussion about their own experiment. Even Bliss, who had never paid attention to a teacher in her life, seemed to be having more fun than usual, swinging backwards and forwards in her seat, and making jokes with Jake. Nerris sighed and, seeing nothing better to do, resorted to joining Liam in his clock-watching session to pass the time. *I can't wait till this is over*, she thought.

After what felt like a millennium, the class were dismissed, and everyone piled through the door at once. The five friends quickly found each other and stepped to the side of the classroom so as to avoid the mob of people charging outside. It was only when enough quiet had been obtained for them to hear each other whispering that they started to talk.

'Ready for this, *Li Li*?' Bliss taunted at once, her eyes alight with twisted pleasure.

Liam was, by this point, unable to form a decent comeback. Instead, he settled for a low, pitiful moan.

Lucy looked at him with very Nerris-style sympathy. 'D'you want me to come with you?' she asked. 'For moral support?'

Still unable to talk, Liam could only grunt and nod in response, his expression one of pure terror. Once again, the others shared knowing and amused glances, while Lucy glared at them reproachfully, heat radiating from her cheeks.

'C'mon,' she told Liam hastily. 'No time like the present, right?'

'Good luck!' Sherona grinned, patting Liam on the arm with mock compassion, before running off with the others, joking heartily about the look on his face.

After watching them till they were out of sight, Liam turned to Lucy, his skin suddenly the colour of curdled milk. 'I can't do this,' he whispered meekly, his whole body trembling violently, 'I just can't do it, Lu!'

'You have to!' she insisted, 'I never thought I'd say this, but Bliss is right! Besides, don't you think it's worse to string her along than tell her the truth?'

He appeared to be struggling against the urge to retch, but he swallowed hard and shook his head. 'If I tell her, she'll kill me; probably literally!'

'And if you don't, what's she gonna do then? D'you seriously think she's just going to leave you alone after a while? Something tells me that'd be a little too much to hope for!' She felt herself squirm inwardly as she spoke, though she was unsure why. Surely her words had been directed only at him; surely he was the only person they related to? Thinking back to the sleepover she had shared with him and the others a few months ago, and how desperately she had wished that Rebecca would stop chasing after him, Lucy's feeling of guilty embarrassment heightened dramatically.

Blushing fiercely, she made herself focus on the task at hand. 'I don't see her anywhere. Are you sure we'll find her here?' she asked, looking around the quickly emptying playground for any sign of Bamforth approaching.

Liam let out a grim bark that almost resembled laughter. 'Oh, she'll be here,' he told her firmly. 'Trust me. As soon as she sees me with you, she'll want to get in on the action. In fact, she'll probably think we're together or something!' He laughed again and she found herself becoming instantly infuriated. What was so funny about the idea of them being an item? *Stop it,* she snapped mentally, praying that her crimson face had not given Liam any sign of this latest thought, *Of course he's laughing; it's a totally ridiculous idea!* She cleared her throat, doing her utmost to ignore the tiny voice now echoing through her head as it told her that Liam's actions had hurt. This whole thing was pathetic and demeaning, and – as soon as Liam cleared things with Bamforth – it would all be forgotten. Then, their friendship could return to normal, and everything would go back to how it should be. Very soon, all of this would be over.

As if on cue, Rebecca scurried over and tapped Liam playfully on the shoulder. 'There you are, Li Li!' she exclaimed. Her tone was clearly intended to be flirtatious, but, in reality, it made her sound as though she had been sucking helium for at least an hour. The unnaturally high pitch with which she spoke was so startling that it made Lucy wince, while Liam jumped about a foot in surprise and whirled round immediately, only for the little residual colour in his cheeks to vanish without trace.

'Er... hi,' he squeaked, petrified. 'I um... hoped to catch up with you sometime.'

'Reeeeally? That's soooo totally weird! I've, like, been reeeeally wanting to see you for, like, ever!' Giggling, she leaned in close and laid her hands on his shoulders, her eyes sparkling with an unnerving and sickening pleasure.

Stumbling backwards, Liam tried and failed to free himself from her clutches. 'Becks, listen,' he stuttered, 'I... I have to talk to you about... about... *this!*'

'Go ahead,' she purred, pressing herself into his chest and tightening her grip, 'I'm all ears!'

'You see, the... the thing is that I... I... um... er...' He glanced over at Lucy for guidance, only to discover that she was suddenly standing a long way off – a deadly expression on her face.

Rebecca pulled him back towards her – a hungry look in her eye that mimicked that of a ravenous wolf about to strike down its prey. The two of them were now within such a short distance of each other that her rapid, shallow breath was filling his ears like the hiss of a poisonous snake.

A bizarre and horrifying thought occurred to him as Rebecca dragged her talon-like hands through his hair. *I am about to be devoured by a wild animal.*

'Rebecca!' he shouted, fighting for all he was worth to escape his gut-twisting quandary. 'Rebecca, listen, I want to—'

'Shh,' she whispered, pressing her finger firmly against his lips to silence him, 'I totally know what you're saying, Li Li.'

And, before he could protest, she kissed him full on the lips, forcing her tongue over his, so that he could not breathe. Like a drowning sailor, he desperately attempted to pull away, but he found himself almost paralysed by shock and unable to combat her efforts. Instead, he was left with no choice but to let her continue.

When at last he was able to inhale the fresh, sweet air around him once more, Liam was struck dumb with bewilderment and revulsion. His mouth hung open like that of a goldfish stranded on dry land, while Rebecca continued to beam at him, her scarily perfect teeth glinting in the sunlight.

'Enjoyed that, huh?' she asked. 'Well, it was, like, about time one of us made a move!' She traced her finger around his lips and kissed him again, though Liam was thankful that, this time, contact was brief. Giggling in her trademark style, Rebecca looked at him with shining eyes. 'So, like, this is totally official now? Yay!' Squealing with joy, she jumped up and down in excitement before checking her watch. 'Look, I'm reeeeally sorry but I've gotta go, I'll see you tomorrow, baby!'

Before Liam could think of any response, she trotted away.

The sheer confusion he felt at what had just happened took a while to subside and, when it finally did, it was replaced with an almost overpowering desire to vomit.

What have I done?

A groan ripped through his body, and he was suddenly terrified he might burst into tears. Why was it so hard for him to tell Rebecca where to go? Bliss could certainly have done it; Sherona, Lucy, Zack and even Nerris would probably be able to if the situation called for it. What was it about his brain that made him so ridiculously oversensitive at times like this? It only brought him strife, so why couldn't he bite the bullet? Groaning loudly, he covered his face with his hands.

Now there was no escape. Bamforth had finally succeeded in entangling him in her spider's web of obsession, and he was not tough enough to fight his way out. In Rebecca's head, the kiss had cemented their relationship, and she would be telling everyone that he was her boyfriend before long. It was impossible to consider crushing her hopes now, and so he was left with just one option: play along until she got bored and ended it, however long that might take. Despair flooded into him from all directions, and it was all he could do not to scream. Head bent and fists clenched at his sides, he began to trail slowly home, tripping over his own feet several times as he went. The same question tormented him like a beat of a broken record: *What have I done?*

So deep and all-consuming was Liam's sorrow that he almost forgot about Lucy. When he turned to look for her, she had gone.

THIRTY-SIX

The silence in the motel room was now so loud that Nick could barely hear himself think.

Things had been this way since Delilah and Layna had returned from the Brand residence, no longer accompanied by Oliver, and had explained to the other two what had happened. Immediately, the cell had moved to a new base, taking minimal supplies with them. After Nick had informed the rest of the FF of the events that had taken place, the four of them had entered into a state of siege. By now, they were all growing pretty tired of it.

Nick, in particular, found the sense of confinement impossible to bear. The thirst for progress that had overtaken him the night he met the starving girl on the street had not yet been quenched, and the recent failure of Harper, Johns and Wafer to gather anything of use during their stake-out had only intensified his maddening desire. Burying their heads in the sand, as they were now, seemed to him the most inexcusable display of cowardice humanly possible. In his mind, every second spent brooding over

Oliver's arrest was a second that could have been spent avenging him – making the Insiders pay for what they had done.

For Wafer personally, Nick felt not loyalty, but contempt. He even harboured a secret sense of relief about the fact that he had been so effectively taken out of his way. The involuntary departure of his closest collaborator meant that Luke had been forced to temporarily rein in his attempts to start a mutiny, thereby giving Nick a momentary reprieve, something Cookson relished wholeheartedly. His desire to retaliate against what had happened was born solely from a need to show his enemies that the FF was not about to back down and that any attempt to force them to do so would only add fuel to their destructive fire. Aside from this, he was determined to show the rest of the FF that he was just as resilient as his father had been and that he, too, deserved his chance to lead. How was he supposed to prove his worth by skulking around doing nothing? Shaking his head, he turned abruptly to face the rest of his cell.

'This is ridiculous!' he announced. 'We've gotta do something to stop them getting away with this! Girls, tell me *exactly* what happened when Oliver was arrested; I want *all* the details.'

Delilah, who was lying on her bed in a pattern resembling a splayed starfish, sat up, and rolled her eyes moodily. 'We've been through this about a million times. What more d'you wanna know?'

He glared at her and shrugged. 'I dunno, but the tiniest thing could make a difference here. Look, just run the whole thing past me again, OK?'

She muttered sourly under her breath, but, out of boredom more than anything else, nodded her head slowly. 'All right. We got there at about eight o'clock, when it was already getting dark. Lay had got there before us, but hadn't seen anything interesting, right?' She glanced at Layna – who nodded to confirm the facts – before looking back at Nick and continuing. 'So, we started to set up. Everything was normal for a bit, and then they, the Insiders, came charging towards us out of nowhere. We were outnumbered two to one, so we had to get out of there. Lay and I were ready to leave in two seconds flat, but Oliver wouldn't budge. I dunno what possessed him, but he just kept shooting. We both told him to get a grip, but he wouldn't listen. Then they were on top of him, and we had to run back to you guys before they got to us too. You know the rest.'

Nick felt immense frustration flare up inside him and his voice rose angrily as he came closer to her. 'That's it? That's all either of you can remember? *How the bloody hell is that gonna help?*'

'I dunno, do I?' Delilah shouted back, folding her arms defensively. 'I was a little busy then, believe it or not. I wasn't exactly taking ruddy notes!'

There was a tense silence, and then Nick exhaled loudly, as though trying to release his discontent into the air around them. 'OK,' he sighed. 'If you're sure, then we'll just have to work with it. Any ideas?'

He looked eagerly around the room at the others, but felt his hope fade as both Delilah and Layna shrugged and shook their heads. Left with no other option, he turned his gaze on Luke, who was sprawled in a rickety armchair by the door.

'Well?' Nick asked.

Knight's eyes narrowed, and he got slowly and deliberately to his feet, appearing almost bored.

'Well?' Cookson repeated, staring him down.

Luke took a long pause, enjoying the feeling of keeping his enemy on tenterhooks. Though this sensation was occurring more and more frequently as time passed, the joy he experienced each time remained undiminished. Smiling deviously, he watched Nick's self-control start to slip away from him, replaced by a deep aggravation that was thoroughly entertaining to behold. *Just a little longer,* he thought, his leer widening. *Make him wait just a little longer.*

He was only made to end his game when he became aware that Layna was frowning quizzically at him. Keen to avert any suspicion that may be creeping into her mind, he spoke at last. 'Well, obviously, we can't rush into anything – not if we wanna avoid joining him in there. Freedom Fighter survival law number one, remember? Besides, if you ask me, he might not be worth risking our necks for. Doesn't it strike anyone else as odd that the Insiders knew exactly where you were going to be? Oliver wasn't supposed to be on that sting at all – it was *him* that insisted on it. Who's to say he's not the little rodent we've been digging for?'

'Bloody hell' muttered Delilah. 'If you're right then we have to get out of here. We're not safe if he might have blabbed about our location.'

'Let's do it.' Nick forced himself to sound business-like and controlled. 'We should wait till it's dark before we make a move, though; we don't want anyone to tail us.'

'Right,' Layna agreed, 'but we should start packing everything up now; that way we'll be ready to leave as soon as the opportunity arises. That'll make the transition a whole lot more efficient.'

Nick grinned at her and nodded. 'Looks like you're finally learning the way things work on this side of the fence, Layna.'

She smiled back uncertainly. 'I guess I am.'

As she spoke, a surge of pleasure ran through her and she found herself thankful for his compliment. Feeling guilty, she hurriedly got to her feet. 'C'mon then, let's get to it,' she urged them all.

The rest of the cell nodded in agreement, and it wasn't long until everything they collectively possessed was stacked outside the door in a variety of ramshackle carrycases.

Stepping back to admire the group's efforts, Delilah stretched and glanced outside onto the darkening street. 'I reckon we can head off now. Does anyone mind stopping at the pub before we find a new place? After all that work, I need to revive myself.'

'I'll second that,' Nick replied, 'but you can go ahead if you want. I'm just going to give this place the once over, make sure there's no fingerprints or anything left behind. You can never be too careful with Insiders.'

Delilah, Layna and Luke all headed for the doorway, and once it had closed behind them Nick set to work. The silence that now filled the room was a much more comfortable one than its predecessor, and the effect was that he found himself relaxing. Clearly, he had read far too much into Luke's earlier actions. The man was dangerous, no question, but he wasn't a fool. Delilah was an excellent fighter and if she sensed even the slightest abnormality in Luke's behaviour towards him, she would definitely make her displeasure felt. Even Layna, whom Nick had so far regarded as the weakest member of the cell, had begun demonstrating an intelligence that could certainly come in useful should he require an ally. *Anyway,* he reminded himself as he carefully combed the bed frames for incriminating evidence, *it'd be impossible for him to do anything without help; he said so himself when you first found out about his plan.* At this thought, he allowed himself to smile.

'Enjoying yourself there, are you?' asked a chilling and familiar voice from behind him.

Sickness swelled in his guts, and he turned slowly to face his foe. 'What d'you want?' he snarled.

Luke chuckled; the sound as icy as an arctic wind. 'I thought I'd wait for you. I want a word.'

'Have two,' Nick hissed. 'Piss off!'

'Oh, feeling braver today, are you? Shame I can't let that last.' With a lightning-quick pace, he sunk his fist into Nick's stomach, so that he fell to the ground, doubled over in pain and spluttering with surprise.

Again, Luke cackled mercilessly. 'That's better. Back to the natural hierarchy – just the way I like it.' Taking a step closer, he seized the front of Nick's shirt and dragged him to his feet. 'Don't worry, this is only going to be a brief discussion.'

Furious and petrified in equal measure, Nick yanked himself free and held Luke's gaze with contempt. 'You've got that right; it's already over.' As quickly as possible, he made to move forwards, but Luke's reflexes were too quick for him, and he soon found himself pinned uncomfortably against the back wall.

'Not so fast' Luke spat, his saliva dampening Nick's face. 'Though, I admit, I have to give you credit for trying. Unfortunately, that's another thing I can't abide, so I sincerely hope you won't attempt it again.' The malice in his face intensified, and the next words he spoke were sharp as pins. 'We wouldn't want you to get hurt now, would we?'

'Just get to the point, will you?' the other man muttered, giving up on his escape attempt and glaring at his tormentor with every ounce of loathing he could muster.

Luke leered down at him, the satisfaction of yet another victory flooding his face in a second. 'With pleasure,' he answered, 'I don't want to waste any more time here than necessary. My point is this: watch your back. I know how happy you are that the idiot Wafer is locked up; I could see the relief in your face the second the girls came back. I suppose you're stupid enough to think I'll give up now that he's out of the picture. Hate to be a killjoy but think again. I always intended to sever ties with Oliver eventually, you know; it just happened rather sooner than I expected. It's not an issue, though; there are plenty of other agents who'll be more than happy to help me out, many of them stronger, cleverer and a hell of a lot more skilled than he ever was. You'd better not get too comfy at the top, Cookson, because it won't be long before you come crashing down.' With these terrible words, he slammed Nick against the wall and released his grip so that Nick landed on the ground with an ominous thud.

Winded, Nick bit down involuntarily on his bottom lip so hard that blood trickled from his mouth.

'You're so pathetic,' Luke taunted venomously as he watched.

For several moments, all Nick could do was remain totally motionless, being far too dazed to react in any other way. When his shock eventually began to wane, he raised a trembling hand to his lips and wiped the blood away. His father had shown him that to emerge from battle injured was to emerge weakened, and, whatever happened, he was determined to heed those teachings.

Getting to his feet, he spoke in a shaky yet imperious voice. 'You are going to pay for that, Private Knight; mark my words.'

'I'd like to see you try, *Commander*,' his enemy told him, mimicking his tone with a melodramatic emphasis, 'really, I would.' Laughing wickedly to himself, Luke turned on his heel and strode away.

Nick had no option but to follow his lead, praying that he looked semi-normal. If Layna and Delilah noticed his weakness, he would never forgive himself, for he knew how bitterly disappointed in him his father would've been, had any fault been apparent. *'Whatever happens, appear strong. Always appear strong,'* he reminded himself, mentally quoting his father as he walked. So focused was he on recalling his childhood life lessons, that he didn't notice someone else had entered the room until they started to speak.

'What's going on, you two?' Layna quizzed, her gaze travelling past Luke to rest on Nick, lingering on the crusty wound visible upon the lower lip of the latter. *'What the hell happened in here?'*

'Nothing.' The reply Nick gave was immoderate and expressionless, giving Layna the impression of some kind of state-of-the-art robot. 'We were just finishing up.'

Unwilling to let the matter of his injury go unanswered, she continued to pursue her questioning. 'How did you do that?' she asked, gesturing to the cut, 'It wasn't there when we left.'

'I fell over, that's all. Dead stupid of me.'

Frowning, she shook her head. 'It looks worse than that to me. Are you sure that—'

'He's fine,' Luke interrupted harshly, 'I was there; I saw it. Just drop it, OK?'

Taken aback, Layna turned to face him with narrowed eyes. 'I was just asking; there's no need to go off on one. If you're sure you're OK, Nick, Delilah's getting impatient; she sent me back here to hurry you up.' She rolled her eyes and grinned. 'You know what she's like.'

Somehow, Nick managed to smile back. 'Yeah, tell me about it. We'd better get a move on before she decides to really lose it on us!'

As soon as the subject of Nick's damaged lip had been closed, Luke's muscles had relaxed considerably and the cocky smirk that came so naturally to his face was borne once more. 'Definitely,' he agreed, 'let's go.'

As the three of them made their way out of the building towards the local pub, Layna's brow furrowed once more, and a peculiar feeling of unease came over her. The gash in Nick's lip had looked very deep for one obtained via tripping up, and his response to her concerns had definitely been odd. Something about the expression Luke's face had worn also unsettled her. It had been sour and disdainful, to say the least, and had a distinctly sinister edge to it. Chilled by the image, she tried to push her anxieties away.

Luke and Nick got on perfectly well as far as she could see, and, aside from her contradictory gut feeling, the story of Nick's fall checked out fine. *You've spent too much time at the FF,* she thought to herself. *It's made you suspicious of everything. At least, with Oliver under suspicion, they're off the scent. Just relax for a while, everything's fine.*

✎

Despite her determination to ignore her instincts, Layna was unable to entirely shake off her edginess over the course of the evening. The inclination that something about the events of the day weren't kosher continued to play on her mind, and she found it impossible to suppress the sense of foreboding that pressed in on her heart as she attempted to go to sleep later that night. Sighing, she rolled over and tried to focus on something else. *Stop being stupid,* she told herself. *You've got enough to think about without adding fantasy to the mix.*

Unbeknownst to her, the lack of Nick's customary sleep talking in a room two floors below demonstrated that she was not the only one who sleep was eluding in the darkness.

THIRTY-SEVEN

'*What were you thinking?*' Zack exclaimed, staring at Liam with a look of utmost horror on his face. 'Why the hell didn't you say something, *do* something to stop her? I thought you said you'd *never* go out with her!'

'I did! I don't *want* to date her, but I've got no choice,' Liam wailed despairingly. 'She already thinks we're an item, so there's nothing I can do. I'll just have to wait a while until I think of a plan to end it; that won't be too bad.'

'Mate, are you kidding? It'll be the worst thing that's happened to you in your whole life! Here's a plan: just get a restraining order.' He fell into the chair behind his desk and shook his head in disbelief. 'You've really messed this up.'

'You think I haven't realised that?' Liam snapped, his temper flaring, 'I feel like a complete prat!' Groaning loudly, he took a deep breath and changed the subject. 'I didn't come here for a lecture; I've had enough of that from the others. Is Lu in? I haven't seen her since – you know – that day.'

'She's in her room, I think. I warn you, though, she's in a pretty black mood.'

Liam's stomach muscles tightened, and he felt a sudden surge of guilt. 'Really? Why… why's that then?' he asked anxiously.

Zack shrugged. 'I dunno. All anyone can get out of her at the moment is "none of your business!" If you want to have a crack at getting her to talk, then, by all means, be my guest. That said, I advise you to be careful.'

Liam nodded grimly. 'Right. Wish me luck.'

'I'm the one who needs luck; I've got to try to explain to Mrs Pollington that the whole of The Inside does not answer to her every whim – *not* an easy task!'

Both boys laughed, but then they remembered what they had to face and the sound died at once. 'Good luck,' they mumbled to one another as they parted ways, each sure that they needed the support more than the other.

As Liam ascended the stairs to reach Lucy's room, he searched his mind for the right words to say when he saw her. The mere notion that she had witnessed what had taken place with Rebecca was enough to make him squirm with embarrassment, and he was certain that any attempt to justify his actions would result in him becoming hopelessly tongue-tied. If Lucy's mood was as dreadful as Zack said it was, then it was virtually a given that she would not tolerate any mistakes made on his part. With a whimper of shameless self-pity, he resigned himself to the imminent humiliation that now reared its ugly head, and knocked tentatively on her bedroom door. 'Lu,' he called warily. 'Can I come in?'

There was silence from behind the door, and he felt the now familiar sinking sensation he had experienced so often over the past few days. 'Please?' he asked beseechingly, 'I want to talk to you.'

After another pause, her quiet and begrudging voice finally came back to him. 'If you must.'

Relieved at finally being granted an audience with her, Liam hastily entered the room before she could change her mind. As soon as he was over the threshold, he saw her spread out on her bed, staring moodily up at the ceiling. 'Hi,' he greeted her, smiling as widely as he could. 'Long time no see.'

She gave a non-committal grunt of acknowledgement and resumed her silence, neither inviting him to continue nor providing him with a conversational lifeline.

Liam cleared his throat uneasily and went on. 'Look, Lu, about the other day, with Rebecca—'

'Oh, I don't want to revisit that particular moment in time, thanks,' she interrupted quickly, 'if it's all the same to you. I think I saw all I needed to at the time. Anyway, what's it got to do with me?'

'I just want to clear the air, that's all. The whole thing was really humiliating for the both of us and—'

'Not for you, I shouldn't think,' she countered with a strange, sardonic laugh. 'You looked to me like you were rather enjoying yourself.'

'*What?* Where the hell did you get that idea from? The whole thing was bloody torture!' As though to prove the point, he shuddered violently as he spoke.

Seeing this seemed to soften Lucy slightly, and she at last sat up to look him in the eye. 'Seriously?' she asked hesitantly.

'Yeah!' he replied emphatically, seized by the sudden hope that all may not be lost. '*Totally.*'

Sighing with relief, his friend leapt to her feet and came over with a huge smile on her face. 'You told her where to go, then?'

Immediately, his elation drained away to be replaced with a sickening sense of shame, 'I… I…' he stuttered, 'not exactly.'

A deep frown line slowly crept onto her forehead, and the happiness in her expression seemed to wither like a dying flower. 'What d'you mean?'

'You saw what she was like; she wouldn't listen to a word I said! How was I supposed to explain to her that I didn't like her that way when she barely gave me time to draw breath? She's just assumed we're together, and I… I… I haven't had the time to correct her yet.'

For a minute, the mystified look on her face appeared frozen there – her eyes wide and mouth slightly open – then, as though in slow motion, the expression morphed into one of bitter resentment and, to Liam's bewilderment, profound disappointment. 'Oh,' she whispered, her voice tighter and much more serious than usual, 'I see.'

They regarded each other in tense and uncomfortable silence for what felt like forever before, at length, Liam made a timid attempt to break it. 'You OK, Lu?'

The undisguised plea in his voice and the puppy-dog look in his eyes made Lucy feel instantly warmer towards him, and guilt for the way she had behaved stabbed through her at once. Looking straight back at him, she plastered a smile on her face and nodded her head. 'Course I am.'

Her words had the desired effect of putting Liam's conscience at ease. 'Good,' he replied with a relieved grin, 'you had me worried there for a second.'

Shrugging, she laughed off his concern. 'I'm fine. Wanna go downstairs and see Zack for a bit?'

'OK,' Liam agreed, 'if he can get away from Pollington. He was just about to phone her when I came up here.'

At first, Lucy felt sympathetic, but then – imagining her friend's face as he attempted to handle the full-on moaning machine that was Mrs Pollington – she giggled in spite of herself. 'Poor him!'

The pair of them left the room in much higher spirits than those with which they had entered, and even Lucy found her pleasure was genuine. Liam may be seeing Rebecca for the time being, but the "relationship" was bound to end sooner or later. She wasn't even sure why she cared about it so much. Liam's love life was his own to control and had absolutely nothing to do with her. When Zack had begun dating, she hadn't made a big deal out of it at all; why should things be different with Liam? *But then,* she mused, *Layna is a fully fledged member of the human race*. Shaking her head and chuckling to herself, she tried to focus on the positives. If she was sure of anything, it was that life would never be dull with Rebecca Bamforth around.

THIRTY-EIGHT

'You know,' Layna said thoughtfully, linking her fingers with Zack's as, a few hours later, they walked up the street towards a quaint coffee shop on the corner, 'it's actually quite weird how little we know about each other.'

Surprised, her boyfriend released her hand as they arrived at their destination, frowning slightly as he held the door open for her. 'You think?'

'Yeah. It feels like all we ever seem to talk about is serious stuff, like the FF and things. We've never actually talked about our families, have we?'

A muscle tightened in Zack's jaw as they entered the coffee shop, and he shook his head slowly, as though reluctant to respond. 'No, I guess we haven't.'

They sat down, and she took his hand across the table, smiling at him eagerly.

'So, tell me about the rest of the McGregor clan,' she urged him.

'You first,' he replied. 'My family tree is seriously

boring!' He laughed. 'If yours is half as wonderful as you are, then I'm all ears.'

'That's one hell of a dodgy line, but if that's what you want, then I guess I can oblige. My family are absolutely humiliating, but they certainly aren't boring; I can say that for them. Just promise you won't treat me differently when I tell you about them.'

'I promise,' he assured her, 'If you get this stuff over with now, we never have to discuss them again if you don't want to.'

Swayed, Layna took a deep breath. 'All right,' she agreed 'but if you laugh I swear I will kill you! Mum used to be a glamour model back before I was born, but she gave that up years ago, thank God. Now she spends most of her time partying it up and wallowing in Dad's hard-earned money. So long as she has at least two new designer handbags per week, she's happy. The rest of us mere mortals take a definite back seat. Dad does sod all about it, of course; he's too terrified of her to even attempt it. Then there's Lois, my older sister. She's like a tornado in the middle of an empty field, the way she tears through life, taking out anything and everything in her path. She somehow managed to survive to her eighteenth birthday, but Lord knows how. Mum and Dad are endlessly threatening to kick her out, but she always finds a way to talk them out of it. It's a wonder she was never expelled from school and she hasn't got a hope in hell of going to uni. Nowhere in its right mind would take her on. My parents are so ashamed of her they contemplated sending her to The Outside!'

Zack breathed in sharply. 'Really? That's so harsh!'

'I know,' she agreed seriously. 'They've stopped going on about it since I... you know. I don't think they view the place as a holiday camp any more.' A dour look came over her face and she sighed deeply. 'At least me going there was good for something.'

He studied her face worriedly. 'Is it really getting to you? You know you don't have to do anything you don't want to; we can get you out of there at a moment's notice if necessary and...' he petered out when he noticed how close to laughter she was, 'What?'

'It's just... you're so good to me. You worry worse than my father, and, let me tell you, he could worry for The Inside. It's just so sweet!' She leaned over and brushed his lips with her own, a grin on her face. 'I'm fine though, really. It helps a lot of people to have a mole in the FF, and if I manage to make Inside life better somehow, then I'm proud of that.' She shrugged her shoulders. 'It's just hard work.'

'You need comfort food,' Zack decided with a smile, passing her the menu, 'Take your pick.'

Beaming, she scanned the choices quickly. 'I'm paying this time, OK?' she told him as she did so. 'No arguing!'

He sighed, but, noticing the determination he so often saw in her eyes, recognised that her mind was made up, 'OK, if you insist.'

'I *do* insist!' She pushed the menu back across the table towards him. 'Now, what d'you fancy?'

'I'm not hungry, thanks,' he answered and once again his expression became mildly strained. Layna looked a little concerned, but he grinned to reassure her, and she relaxed.

'All right' she agreed as she got up, 'if you're sure.'

He watched her make her way towards the counter, with a wide smile on his face, but it faded from view after only a few seconds. The sheer scale of the love he felt for her was unbelievable, and he wanted nothing more than to honour her trust in him with a matching degree of honesty. How could he do that when he was keeping such a huge secret from her? If she had set her heart on finding out about his family, then it was an impossible wish that he'd be able to avoid mention of them forever, but how could he explain things to her? *I can't,* he thought wretchedly, *I just can't do it.*

For the ten years he had known them, he had not divulged the information in question to his friends, and the idea of confiding in Layna now felt horribly disloyal. Still, the others had never shown more than a passing interest in his home life, and he had never yet needed to lie to them outright to protect what he wanted so desperately to conceal. Should Layna resume her previous questioning, which doubtless she would, then that was what he would have to do to her. Even thinking of committing such an act brought out in him painful surges of despair. What was he going to do?

'Baby, are you OK?' Layna enquired softly, pulling him sharply from his upsetting thoughts, 'What's wrong?'

'Huh? Oh, nothing; I… I was just thinking.' Searching frantically through his brain, he tried to come up with a simple ploy with which to distract her from the topic of their earlier discussion. 'Are you sure you're safe to be away from the FF right now?'

Both relief and exasperation appeared on her face at once, and she slid back into her seat. 'Of course I am! D'you really think I'd leave the rest of my cell if I wasn't one hundred per cent sure it was safe?'

'Well, no, I… I suppose not, but just say—'

'Relax, OK? I know what I'm doing and, besides, I haven't seen you in ages; I've missed you like hell.'

'I've missed you too, but—'

'I got clearance from the head of the FF himself before I came out, so just stop worrying and enjoy yourself! God knows you have enough on your plate with work without stressing about me as well. Now, enough about that, why don't you tell me about your folks now?'

Her words sent his heart racing, and it felt as though a stone the size of a beach ball had dropped into his stomach. 'I…' he began, dreadfully aware of how much his voice was shaking, 'you… you don't want to know about them.'

'Yes, I do!' she replied, looking surprised, 'I swear I won't take the mick. Can they really be any more mortifying than my lot?'

'Trust me; you *really* don't want to know!'

'Trust *me* – I really, really *do* want to know!'

He knew for a fact that whatever he said would have no bearing whatsoever on her point of view, but he was also sure that if he told her his secret, she would turn her back on him. Unable to face the prospect of losing her, he found himself shouting, 'WHY CAN'T YOU JUST DROP IT, LAYNA? It's none of your business anyway and… and…' His legs trembled as he leapt to his feet, uncontrollable panic clouding his brain like a toxin. 'And I'm sick and tired of you continuously pushing me over it!' Intense pain shot through him as he saw the effect his poisonous words were having on her, but he found himself unable to stop. He pushed as hard as he could against the table, causing an almighty screech as it scraped several centimetres across the floor, drawing every eye in the place towards them.

Stunned and perplexed by the way he was acting, Layna, too, got up from her seat, and said in a gentle and soothing voice. 'Calm down. What's up with you today, hmm?'

Propelled by his terror, he turned away and stalked out of the building, the sound of his roaring blood very nearly drowning out the cry of utter despair now threatening to explode out of him. What in God's name was he doing? Layna was the best thing that had ever happened to him, and here he was throwing the relationship away. Tears sprang to his eyes as he sprinted down the street, with the image of Layna's hurt and puzzled face torturing him relentlessly as he went.

✗

Only when his legs were crying out for relief from the self-imposed agony ripping through them did he finally collapse onto the nearest bench and bury his face in his hands. There was no way in the world she would continue things with him after this, and he certainly couldn't blame her. Everything he should have told her echoed unbearably through his head and he knew that his outburst was going to haunt him for the rest of his life. *Why?* he screamed at himself in his head, dizzy with heart-wrenching regret. *Why did you do that?*

Earlier, the summer evening had seemed pleasantly bright and warm to him, but it had suddenly grown as cold as if it were midwinter, and every scrap of light appeared to have been swallowed up by a pitch-black cloak of sadness. Shivering, he drew his arms around himself and waited for the world to end.

'There you are. For a minute then I thought I'd never find you! Don't scare me like that, all right?'

Hardly daring to believe what he was hearing, he raised his head and stared at the figure in front of him, open mouthed. 'Layna!' he croaked in disbelief. 'What... what're you doing here?'

'What d'you think, genius? I want to talk to you.' She sat down beside him, and draped her arm round his shoulders, pulling him as close as she could. 'Tell me what's wrong.'

Shaking his head, he pulled away sharply. 'Nothing. I just… I…' He exhaled, exasperated. 'It's too complicated to explain. You wouldn't understand.'

'I would if you'd just try to talk to me! Or at least, if I can't understand, I can be there for you. Please, Zack, just tell me what's going on.' Imploringly, she looked deep into his eyes, her expression intensely sorrowful. 'Don't you trust me?' she whispered unhappily,

Gigantic waves of guilt washed over him as she spoke, and his heart filled with yet more misery. 'It isn't that, I promise you.' Hesitantly, he gritted his teeth and continued as steadily as he could. 'There's… there's something about my family that nobody knows, and it's really important that I keep it under wraps. I've never even told my best mates. If anyone was to find out…' he trailed off, the unimaginable horror of that possibility too severe to put into words. He cast his eyes downwards, and his shoulders slumped dejectedly, 'I'm really sorry, but I just can't talk about it.'

'All right,' Layna agreed quietly, taking his hand very firmly in her own, 'I understand. I want you to know something, though.'

'What?'

'Whatever it is, there's no way it can change the way things are between us. I care about you too much for that. I love you to bits, Zackary McGregor.' She held him tight and pulled him in for a kiss.

Gradually, he lost himself in the feel of her and forced his insecurities to the very back of his mind. As the passion of the kiss increased, the dispirited numbness that had encased him since he'd left the café dissolved into non-existence. 'Thank you,' he breathed. 'Thank you.'

They were so near to each other now that their heartbeats merged seamlessly together. The strong and beautiful sound filled Zack's ears, and he experienced a sudden flash of clarity; a relationship that carried this much love could simply not continue when tinged with secrecy and deceit. If he were to show her the same amount of devotion she showed him, then he would have to be entirely open with her, whatever that entailed.

Taking a huge, self-assuring breath, he turned to face her directly. 'Darling,' he announced, 'I can't hide this from you; that isn't right. You deserve honesty, and that's what I'm going to give you. I'm not going to hide from this any more, I'm going to tell you everything.'

THIRTY-NINE

By the time they arrived at Zack's front door, the rain in his head had seeped into reality and it fell upon them like the tears he had been crying only minutes before. With trembling hands, he reached into his pocket to retrieve his house key and slotted it into the lock. 'I warn you,' he told Layna sombrely as he did so, 'you're in for a bit of a shock.'

She nodded and subconsciously increased the strength of her grip on his hand. 'OK.'

There was a clicking sound, telling them both the door was now unlocked. Zack hesitated for a second longer before he pushed it open.

Straightaway, Layna was hit by the overpowering odour of alcohol and cigarettes. Unprepared, she could not help but recoil. Zack gave a grim nod and continued into the house with his head lowered in shame. Layna followed apprehensively and gave a tiny gasp at the sight of the hallway.

It was unlit and she could barely see a thing, but the peeling wallpaper and damp-strewn walls were obvious even in darkness. The interior of this house looked undeniably as though it belonged on The Outside and Layna's stomach flipped over in horror. 'Oh Zack...' she breathed, her voice sounding strangled, 'what on earth...'

'You don't want to know,' he repeated in a whisper, his shaking voice almost incoherent, 'believe me.' Clearing his throat, he tugged lightly at her arm. 'C'mon.'

He showed her into an equally dingy and forbidding living room, littered with signs of poverty and decay.

Stunned, she tried and failed to take it in. *This isn't real,* she thought numbly, her legs turning to jelly beneath her. *It can't be real.* As if in a dream, she broke away from her boyfriend and began to walk slowly around the room, her footsteps echoing loudly throughout the house as she went. There were two dusty photo frames on the windowsill, and she gravitated towards them, seeing them as the smallest flicker of warmth in this cold and frightening place.

The first picture showed a teenage girl standing in a park with her arms around a young boy with scruffy, dark hair.

'Oh my God,' Layna gasped, pointing at the younger child and turning to look at Zack again, 'is that you?'

He nodded, and the ghost of a smile appeared on his face. 'Yep, and that girl is my sister Carla. That photo was taken five years back.'

Layna smiled and looked across at the second photo. Taken on the same day as the first, it depicted Carla and Zack with a group of six other children, clearly their siblings. 'Wow,' Layna murmured, 'there sure are a lot of you!' She looked at the smallest of the photograph's occupants, a girl and a boy who she guessed were aged around one and two, respectively. Zack had pulled them both onto his lap and was clearly tickling them, making them scream with hysterical laughter. 'Ahh,' she crooned with a small smile, 'cute.'

The boy sitting next to Zack caught her eye and she shifted her gaze to look at him. He had to be around the same age and yet his chocolate-brown hair was already slicked back with a generous amount of gel. Though he was smiling for the camera, the expression fell short of reaching his eyes. 'Who's he?' Layna asked curiously, her eyebrows dipping ever so slightly into a frown.

'That'd be me,' said a drawling and unexpected voice, 'but I think the real question here is who're you?'

Jerking round in surprise, Layna saw a fifteen-year-old boy standing on the stairs, peering down at her with an immense level of distrust covering his face. It was the boy she had been studying in the photo, only several years older and much more sullen.

Without even a trace of a smile on his face now, he continued his descent with narrowed eyes. 'Your doing, I presume, brother dearest? After all your talk of never inviting anyone to the house?' He glared at Zack and then sighed theatrically, rolling his eyes with just as much melodrama. 'Though I can't say I'm surprised. It's no secret how much of a disgusting hypocrite you are.'

'Shut your mouth, you jumped-up little sod,' his brother spat. 'You haven't got a bloody clue what's going on!'

'Oh, haven't I?' the newcomer sneered, as he reached the bottom of the stairs and looked from Layna to Zack with a snide leer plastering his pale, pinched face. 'From where I'm standing, it all looks pretty clear.'

Zack blushed with fury and indignation. 'You're way off track, George, and you know it! Anyway, it is no business whatsoever of yours who I invite into this house, got it?'

'It's my house too, and if you can bring home any chick you like, then you've no right to tell me I can't. Who is this bitch anyway? Swanning around here like she owns the place!'

'Don't you dare talk about her like that!'

'I'll talk about her any way I like!' George argued, his eyes flashing malevolently. 'Have you gone completely insane or are you just plain stupid? You can guarantee that if she finds out about us, she'll go crawling to social services with a story so tragic and painful that they'll just *have* to take us into care!' He took a step closer to his brother and – when he next spoke, his voice carrying a distinctly deadly note now – his eyes took on a feral quality that sent icy shock waves through the room. 'Or maybe that's your plan? Maybe you reckon that 'cause you're sixteen and nearly too old for their precious system, getting us caught would be a sure-fire way to keep us out of your hair for good? Yeah, I bet that's it; it's just the sort of self-absorbed thing you would do.'

'WHAT?' Zack roared, now looking as if he was on the verge of hitting his brother, 'WHAT THE EFFING HELL D'YOU TAKE ME FOR?'

'I dunno,' his brother retorted furiously. 'Maybe I see what everybody else seems to be blissfully unaware of – the truth!' He turned his contemptuous wrath on Layna, who was cowering away in fear of what was unfolding. 'You'd better get out of here fast, sweetheart, before I take matters into my own hands. You catch my drift?'

Moving at the speed of light, Zack crossed the room and stepped in front of his girlfriend like a human shield, his arms outstretched. 'You lay just one finger on her and social services will be the least of your worries, *understand*?'

'Oh sure,' George scoffed, his tone positively oozing sarcasm, 'you could totally take me on! Whatever you say, brother.' Then, as though nothing had happened, he strode confidently to the doorway and shot the pair of them an infuriatingly cocky smile. 'Now, I'd love to stay and chat, but I have better things to do than talk to a couple of freaks. I'm off to spend what's left of my evening with some normal people. Don't wait up, I'll be some time.' With that, he swaggered from the room.

What had just taken place was one of the most surreal things that Layna had ever experienced, and her brain was refusing to process what she had just seen. For Zack, acceptance was easier, but the fears that had plagued him ever since Layna had mentioned his family were beginning to come true. Both were shaken to their cores.

For a long time, all either of them could do was lean heavily against each other, listening to the ticking of the clock on the wall, which was the only sound in the otherwise silent world.

'Zack,' Layna whispered eventually, 'what… what was that about? What did George mean when he said I'd be straight to social services if I found out about you? What's going on here, baby? Please help me understand.'

Zack exhaled in exasperation, took her face in his hands and kissed her tenderly upon the forehead. 'Are you sure you want to get involved in this?'

In spite of all that had happened in the past few minutes, Layna managed to give him a shaky laugh. 'I think it's a little bit late to ask me that, don't you?'

Sighing deeply, he hesitated before nodding. 'You're right, and there's no point in putting it off, I suppose.'

They sat down on the threadbare sofa, hands intertwined, and Zack attempted to steady his heart rate by holding her gaze. This had the opposite effect, and he thought his heart may actually escape the confines of his chest if he continued to look into her eyes. Yet he did not look away, for he was certain he would keel over in fear if he did. 'OK, darling,' he whispered. 'It's time to stop playing these games. Time to start talking. Time to come clean.'

Layna felt the grip on her hand tighten. 'It's all right,' she told him soothingly. 'Take your time; there's no rush.'

Zack nodded determinedly, nibbling madly on the corner of his bottom lip. 'I can do this,' he muttered, more to convince himself than her, 'I *can* do this.' Drawing one more trembling breath, he forced himself to go on, with what was clearly a supreme effort. 'My… my father, he's a drug addict; has been for ten years now.' As he spoke, he saw the colour drain from her face and tried to reassure her. 'Don't worry, he doesn't live here any more, but it took a lot to get him to leave.'

The last word caught in his throat, and he had to swallow repeatedly before continuing. 'Four years ago, just after my twelfth birthday, he came home stoned. I've got no idea what he was using, but whatever the hell it was made him go crazy. My sister Molly, who was eight at the time, saw something was up and asked him what was wrong. He went totally berserk!' Zack closed his eyes for a moment, holding back the tears that were now threatening to burst forth. 'He… he… took her by the hair and dragged her to the top of the stairs. We all screamed at him to stop, but he wouldn't let her go; just kept shouting a load of crap about her not trusting him. Then he said she was a waste of space and threw her down the stairs. There was nothing any of us could do to stop him.'

Shaking all over, he pulled one hand free and used it to wipe away his tears, though even a fool could've seen the attempt was useless. 'She… she hasn't been the same since;

she hardly eats and won't say a word to anyone. After Molly got hurt, Dad packed his stuff and left, but once he'd gone Mum took to drink. She's at the pub twenty-four/ seven nowadays. We had all the little ones to support, so Carla moved away to get work. As soon as I was old enough, I dropped out of school and got a job with the Brands. We're all the kids have got now. What George saw the night Molly got injured turned him into a total recluse and so he's as much help as Mum. The others are all too young to work, so...' he shrugged, smothering a desperate sob and clutching at her hands for dear life. 'Please don't tell anyone, Layna,' he begged her through his tears, 'I couldn't bear it if they were taken away from me.'

'Oh baby!' she cried, throwing her arms round his neck and holding him tight, 'I can't believe you've kept this to yourself all this time! It's been weighing down on you so hard and you've never told anybody. Why won't you get any help? There has to be some kind of support out there to—'

'No!' Zack interrupted, the urgency level in his voice escalating. 'No one can find out about this, OK? *No one!* George was right about one thing. If anybody discovers what we're dealing with here the kids'll be straight into care! I promised them that I'd never let that happen and I will *not* break that trust, got it? *Getting help is not an option.*'

The look on her face told him he was shouting and he made himself calm down. 'Sorry, I shouldn't be taking this out on you. I'm just so frantic to keep my family together. You understand that, right?' he asked, his voice anxious and uncertain.

'Of course I do! I get that you don't want to involve any external establishment in this; I mean, who would? What I meant was why haven't you told your friends? Surely it'd be better if you had them to lean on? You guys are tight, aren't you?'

'Yes, of course we are, but I don't want to burden them with my troubles. I didn't want to burden *you* with my troubles and I only did it because I would've had to lie to you if I didn't. With them, that kind of stuff never comes up; things are easier if they stay that way.'

Though she still felt he ought to bring the others in on the secret, as she was certain their involvement would go some way to easing the weight of the insane load that he had carried on his shoulders for so long, Layna had the good sense not to argue with him at a time like this. 'OK, then, this is just between us.'

'Thank you,' Zack answered, the tears on his face finally beginning to dry, 'I knew I could count on you.'

The room fell silent once again, but the difference this time was immeasurable. The quiet now felt comfortable and contented; the air no longer making an attempt to suffocate them.

They remained locked in one another's embrace until a series of thumping sounds upstairs pulled Zack from his reverie. 'That'll be the boys,' he sighed, 'getting bored. I'd better go and make sure they don't tear the place apart.' Getting to his feet, he stretched and gave Layna a wide smile. 'I'll see you tomorrow, yeah?'

She, too, got off the sofa, frowning as she considered his words. 'You know what?'

'What?'

'I think I'll stick around for a bit, if we've still got time before Hurricane George returns!'

Zack laughed. 'OK, but if you think he was a hurricane, wait till you meet James, Stuart, Hugo and Cassie!' He put his hands on her waist and pressed his lips into hers. 'I don't think you've quite realised what you've bought into here!'

'I don't care' she replied with a grin, 'not so long as I have you.' She giggled and stood on her tiptoes to plant a kiss between his eyebrows. 'Besides, I'm involved in this now whether you like it or not!'

Unused to her behaving so cheekily towards him, he found himself laughing in spite of his emotional state. 'All right then, on your own head be it.'

Together, they made their way up the stairs to face whatever carnage lay beyond; both feeling a tumult of mixed emotions surging through them.

Zack's relief at having, at long last, offloaded some of the pressure he had had to cope with was mixed with a deep-rooted concern for both Layna and his family. The more people who got mixed up in this situation, the more high-risk it became. Experience told him that this was an extremely difficult secret to keep, and, well intentioned though she might be, he was doubtful as to whether his girlfriend could manage to remain tight-lipped. *Don't be stupid,* he told himself, *She works as a government mole in one of the most dangerous terrorist groups in the world and she's never even come close to being caught. You can trust her.* He was reassured by the thought and found that his smile reappeared almost immediately. There was no denying that it felt good to have told somebody, and he was sure it had been the right thing to do. Life, he realised, had suddenly become just that little bit more liveable.

Layna was still struggling to come to terms with the evening's events, but her thoughts were much less conflicted than Zack's. The way she saw it, the fact he had decided to open up to her after all this time was a mark of the supreme strength of their relationship and, when she thought of the implications of acquiring the information he had shared with her, she was not filled with apprehension or alarm. Instead, she felt as though an invisible wall that had been driving a wedge between them up to this point had – at long, long last – caved in on itself, thereby leaving the way clear for trust to flow freely to and fro. The light-heartedness she was experiencing seemed wildly inappropriate, given what an emotional battering both of them had taken that day, but she could not suppress the hope that was now firmly taking root inside her. She wholeheartedly believed that the two of them could tackle any problem that came their way, and this, to her mind, was just another learning curve. Whatever happened, they would face it together and whatever setbacks they came up against would only solidify their bond. Whatever happened, they would always have each other.

FORTY

The waves lapped gently against the shore – a new one approaching every time its predecessor receded; the sand newly cleansed with every surge of water. Zack watched the phenomenon time and time again, marvelling at how steady and dependable it was. *If only life was like that,* he mused wistfully, *wouldn't things be simple?*

Laughing at the absurdity of his fantasy, he shook his head and tried to focus on the pleasures of the real world. Had his life been as repetitive and unchanging as the pattern of the waves, then he would never have met Layna or his friends, all of whom were like whirlwinds, seizing hold of anything and anyone they touched and refusing to let go; this, above all else, was what drew Zack to them in such a powerful way. As he thought of them, a grin as wide as the ocean before him broke out across his face, and he raised his eyes to the sunset, the light of which was reflected on the water like a liquid rainbow.

'Hey,' said a cheerful voice from behind him. 'Sorry I'm late.'

'No worries,' he replied, beckoning Layna closer. 'How's it going?'

'Not too bad, though it's been seriously tough with the FF recently. The arrest has everyone fired up and that makes it really difficult to get away when I want to. Luckily, the rest of my cell are out clubbing tonight, and I'm underage, so I had the perfect excuse to escape. I'm glad I did, I can tell you; that lot are completely crazy! The Commander is forever jumping at shadows at the moment, and his second and third in command are both scarily battle-crazed. You'd think there was going to be a war tomorrow or something.' It was a warm evening, but she shuddered as though she was suddenly cold and wrapped her arms around herself anxiously, worrying the corner of her bottom lip as she did so.

Concerned, Zack put an arm around her shoulders and pulled her into an embrace. 'Really finding it hard, huh?' he asked tenderly. 'Harder than you thought?'

She nodded, leaning against his shoulder as though in refuge. 'Uh huh.'

'You know you don't have to do this, right? You can still walk away; it isn't too late.'

He felt a heavy sigh run through her body before she answered, and he had a strong feeling he knew what her response would be before she spoke. Sure enough, it did not take long for him to find that his inkling was well grounded.

'I can't walk away now, Zack,' she told him firmly, 'I'm already too involved. Anyway, there's some stuff going on there I want to check out – weird things. There's this guy, Luke, and he's really dodgy. I don't know what it is, but he just radiates shiftiness. The way the Commander acts around him has changed over the past few months; it's like he's afraid of him or something. It's probably really stupid, but…' She shrugged. 'I guess I'm curious by nature.'

Zack nodded slowly as he digested what she was saying. 'OK, but watch your back. There's no way you can trust anyone from that place; no way.'

'I know that,' she replied reassuringly. 'You don't need to worry about me; I could handle that lot any day.'

'Yeah, but—'

'*But nothing!*' she interrupted, grinning at how overprotective he was, 'I'll be fine! I just needed someone to offload to, that's all. I didn't mean to stress you out.' After kissing him lightly on the cheek, just as she had done when they first met, she, too, turned towards the colourful horizon stretching out ahead of them. 'You were right; it's gorgeous out here.'

Zack found himself once again enveloped in the tranquillity of the place, and he allowed the sea breeze and the salty air to wash over him, as though to sweep away the stress of existence. Her words had reminded him why it was he had asked to meet here. A feeling of peace, which he had rarely experienced in his life, rose up inside him like the warmth of hot chocolate on a bitter winter's night and gently pulled his lips into a smile. 'Yeah,' he agreed, 'it really is.'

A shriek of laughter made them look round, and they spotted a pair of eight-year-old girls chasing each other across the sand, seeming to physically glow with mirth. Laughing, their parents puffed along behind them – broad smiles on their faces. The joy that radiated so strongly from the family unit made Zack's heart miss a beat, and a twinge of jealously crept into the back of his mind. Squashing it back, he took Layna's hand and tried to experience the sight of the family fun for what it was: a truly beautiful thing that, one day, he could find for himself.

'I love this place,' he murmured, 'It's magical, don't you think?'

'Yeah, it is.' Layna agreed. 'I've been living so close to this for so long, and yet I feel like I've never really appreciated it, you know? It's like I'm suddenly seeing it in a new light.'

'I know what you mean. This place has always felt special to me, ever since I can remember, but this just feels perfect.' He used his free hand to gently caress her face, bringing her towards him for a kiss. 'I think I know why.'

'What is it with you and unbelievably clichéd chat up lines?' Layna asked, rolling her eyes. 'They're really cheesy, and if you're expecting me to fall for that sort of thing—'

'What d'you mean "fall for"?' he asked, making his voice sound comically affronted. 'It's the truth!'

'Yeah, right.' She gave him a playful nudge of disbelief. 'Sure it is – just like fairy tales are the truth!'

'I'm serious,' he told her, his dramatics cast aside, 'I'm really glad I could share this place with you, Layna.'

Allowing the sharp, saline tang of the air to fill his nostrils, he let his mind travel back to the night when he had sat in Samuel's office to write the crisis-deflecting speech, and looked out across his homeland towards this very beach. Even then, he had marvelled at how tranquil it was. That tranquillity seemed the only thing that had not changed since then, and this made him appreciate it even more.

The world, he reminded himself now, would always be complicated, and there was nothing anyone could do to stop that being the case. The only thing to be done was to embrace life for all that it was and all that it could be, and take each day as it came.

He had so many unanswered questions – so many things that didn't fit into place – that it was impossible to tell what would occur in the future. One thing was certain though: the road ahead for everybody on The Inside was an unsteady one. The Freedom Fighters continued to jeopardise the lives of so many in their relentless pursuit of destruction and anarchy, and if the way the terrorist group had conducted themselves in the past few weeks was anything to go by, the arrest and imprisonment of one of their agents was more likely to act as fuel for the FF's hate-filled fire than as the preventive force the government had been hoping for.

Imagining the terrible schemes that were perhaps being concocted at this very moment sent sickening shivers of unease through his body, and his heart leapt into his throat every time he thought about it, but – in his heart of hearts – he understood that there was no point dwelling on things that had not yet come to pass. Whatever hardships and dangers he, Layna and the others came up against, they would tackle and overcome them together. No act of terrorism could ever change that. The bond he had with them was a tricky one to navigate, especially when life was as unpredictable as theirs was, but every patient second spent making things work was one it was impossible to regret, and he wasn't going to let anything get in his way. Nothing was ever going to drive a wedge between them – not in a thousand years.

'What're you smiling about?' asked Layna curiously. 'You haven't stopped grinning for the past ten minutes!'

'What? Oh, sorry.' His Cheshire-cat-like grin faded slightly to be replaced with an embarrassed one accompanied by a minor blush. 'Been quite action-packed lately, hasn't it?'

She thought for a moment and realised he was right. The time before she had become a mole in the FF seemed like a dream, and, when she looked back, it was as though she was watching a film or a version of reality that did not belong to her. Nonetheless, she could not feel melancholy about it. Risky as her decision to infiltrate the FF had been, the information it was possible to obtain from such a venture had the potential to change the fortunes of so many innocent people, and that meant her existence had at last been given a real purpose. The sheer volume of changes was, however, incredibly tough to absorb, and if she were honest with herself, it was a struggle to take everything in. "Action-packed" was a phrase that definitely summed things up.

'Yeah,' she agreed, 'it certainly has.' The sea breeze whistled past her and she inhaled deeply, feeling contented and at peace for the first time in weeks. 'We can handle things though, right?'

'Of course we can; we can handle anything.'

Nodding her agreement, she rested her head on his shoulder and closed her eyes. 'Yeah,' she repeated happily, 'you're right.'

For at least five minutes, neither of them said a word, but both knew that speech wasn't necessary. Right now, the only thing they needed to do was make the most of this moment, frozen in time, where they could simply enjoy each other's company as a normal teenage couple would, devoid of the very adult pressures they both had to face. For them, this was true bliss.

They were so wrapped up in the rare moment of perfection that they did not notice that they were being watched.

ACKNOWLEDGEMENTS

This has been an amazing year for me so far – taking something I've been working on for so long and finally releasing it into the world. It amazes me to have got here at last and there are so many people I couldn't have done this without. I give my heartfelt thanks to:

Mum and Dad, without whom literally NONE of this could've happened. Thanks for sticking up for me so much and for not despairing when your little girl first told you she wanted to be a writer – even though I couldn't actually write yet.

To the honorary and actual Hibb Sibs (Kath, Lorna and Dec) for your enthusiasm, hilarity and general brilliance. Love you all SO MUCH!

To the brilliant team at Matador – especially Hannah, Sophie and Fern – for helping me through the wonderful new experience of publishing a book. Your skill and diligence were invaluable.

To Wayne, Matt, Dianne, Sam and Marie. Although you have never met, you all helped me through some of my roughest patches – and I'll always be thankful.

To Cleo for being the best dog, friend and sounding board any writer could ask for. The wags of your tail kept me going when nothing else could!

To my extended family – for being so brilliant for so long, in so many different ways.

Thank you to Nerris, Zack, Lucy, Sherona, Liam and Bliss, my oldest companions, for simply being there when I needed them and stopping me from going completely insane. I love you all and really hope you think I've done the first chapter of your story justice.

Last but not least, thank you to anybody who has the amazing generosity to read this book. It is my deepest wish that you enjoyed reading it as much as I did writing it. Thank you, all of you, from the bottom of my heart.

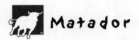

For exclusive discounts on Matador titles,
sign up to our occasional newsletter at
troubador.co.uk/bookshop